I0760666

# PLAYING JENNA

KIERSTEN MODGLIN

KIERSTEN
MODGLIN

Cover Design by Kiersten Modglin
Copy Editing by Three Owls Editing
Proofreading by My Brother's Editor
Formatting by Kiersten Modglin


First Print and Electronic Edition: 2017
kierstenmodglinauthor.com

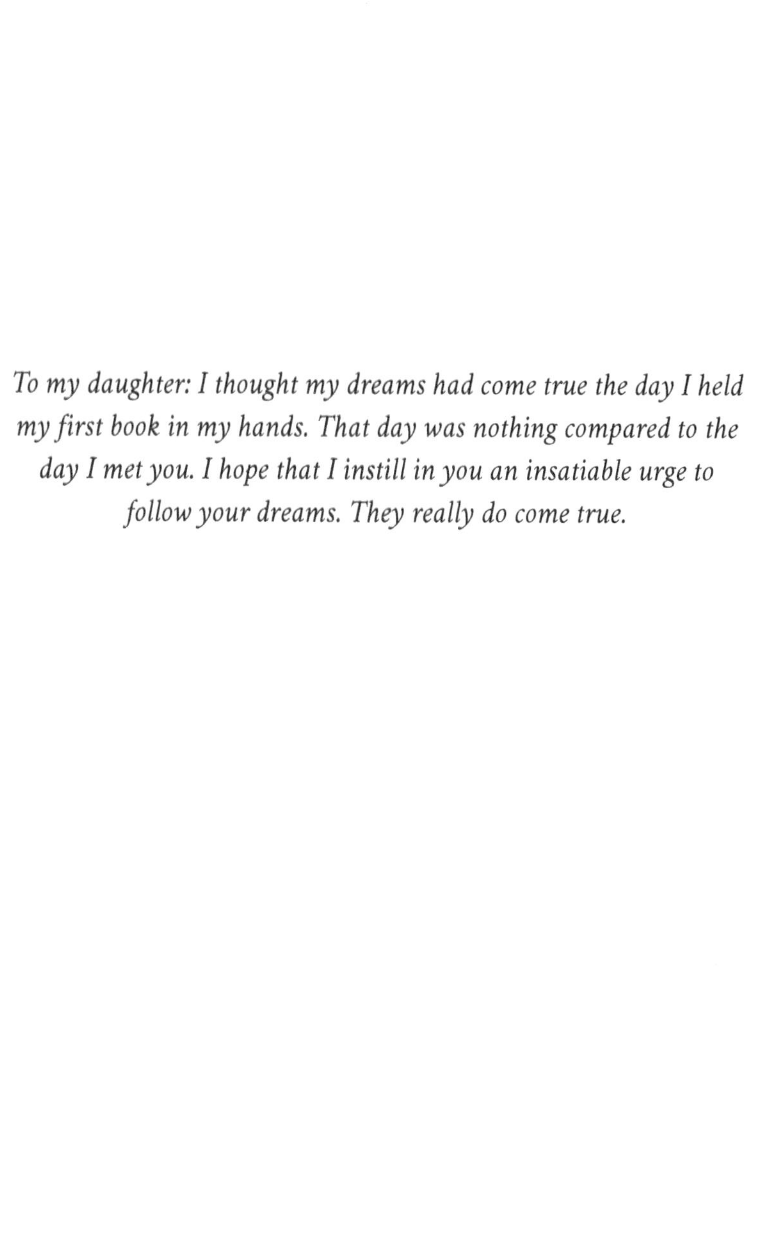

*To my daughter: I thought my dreams had come true the day I held my first book in my hands. That day was nothing compared to the day I met you. I hope that I instill in you an insatiable urge to follow your dreams. They really do come true.*

# MONROE

It wasn't supposed to go this way. She knew that as she stared down at the mess she had made. The thick, dark blood pooled over the white tile of her kitchen, mixing with the puddle of already cold tea. The body lay in front of her, skull so thick with blood that she could hardly see the wound. Her whole body shook with fear and adrenaline, throat tight. *What had she done?*

She would never forget the way the crack had echoed through the empty house or the look on her face as she slammed onto the floor. The panic was plastered there, even now, her mouth gaped open, eyes, even in death, filled with terror.

It was over. Just like that. She was gone. She stepped over a trail of blood as it made its way toward her. The blood was spreading quickly. Everywhere she looked, its sticky darkness was coating the floor. There was just so much. She had to get out of there. She tried to remember, quickly, any place she had touched as she walked through the house, wiping away possible fingerprints as she went.

When she was sure she'd wiped away any trace of evidence that she'd ever been there, she darted out the door, running from the house, and racing toward her car as fast as her legs would carry her. The lone car still remained in the driveway and as she ran past it she expected someone to jump out and stop her. *Try to stop her*. No one did. The dark of the night swallowed her up, concealing her guilty getaway. She panted, her whole body burning, muscles begging for a break, but she refused to quit moving. She couldn't. She had to get out of there before anyone came back. Her arm was dripping blood, her wound wide open. She tried desperately to keep it covered. She hit the edge of the woods quickly, darting through the trees and disappearing into the darkness.

*Disappear.* It was what she had wanted more than anything else. Well...besides revenge.

# MONROE

## BEFORE

Monroe Perry lay awake, listening to the sound of the busy night below her condo. Living downtown had been her husband's idea, one she'd regretted every day since she'd agreed to it.

She tossed and turned, growing more frustrated as her cover seemed determined to entrap her with her every move. Eventually, she gave up, letting out a big sigh and throwing the comforter away from her with gusto.

The cold air hit her quickly, causing cold chills to line her skin. She thought back to the nights, not so long ago, when Colt would've wrapped his arms around her to stop her shivering, his warm breath on her goosebump-lined neck.

She tried to remember the last time he'd done that, though it was hard to remember a last time when she hadn't known it would be *the last time*. Life was funny that way, she realized. When they're gone, moments that once seemed so insignificant suddenly fill you with the regret of not cherishing them more.

Tossing the thought from her head, she stood up, crossing

the room slowly to turn on the light. It was just past three in the morning, she didn't need to be up for nearly eight more hours. Quite frankly, she didn't need to be up at all.

She frowned, staring at the fat, gray cat who lay unfazed at the foot of her bed. "Denny," she called, her voice groggy. He opened his eyes, staring at her with annoyance, but refused to move. Anymore, this cat had the personality of a reclusive, old man. He was constantly grumpy, it seemed, and he did his best to avoid her at all cost. Most nights he wouldn't even make his way into the bedroom until she was fast asleep. "Denny, wake up." She reached over, rubbing her hands over his warm belly. "Come on, you old grump. It's time to get up."

He scowled at her, pressing his paws onto the mattress and arching his back, letting out a noisy yawn. She ruffled his fur, removing her hand only when he swatted it away. When Colt had lived there, Denny loved to sleep between them, cuddling up on their queen bed. Since the day Colt had gone, Denny had taken to sleeping at the foot of the bed every night. It was as if he too would have chosen to leave her if he could.

The day her husband left, Monroe had woken up in the middle of the night too, much like tonight. She'd suffered from insomnia most of her life and it only seemed to get worse as she aged.

That night though, it wasn't her restless mind that had woken her, but rather her husband's restless body. He was whispering softly in his sleep, his eyes fluttering behind closed eyelids, his body tossing and turning under the covers. She sat up, half asleep, and flicked the TV off, in case that was what was causing his discomfort. She threw her leg over his stomach and closed her eyes again, running a hand through his wiry chest hair.

He continued whispering heatedly, indecipherable sounds escaping his mouth. She opened her eyes and pressed her hands onto his cheeks softly, trying to soothe him. He seemed to wake up then, the whispering stopping immediately as he stretched out. He kissed her fingers, pulling them from his face, as he rolled over. He sighed, stretching. She rubbed his back gently, feeling the patches of rough hair that grew sporadically.

"I love you, Jenna," he whispered into the night, his voice coated with sleep. *Jenna.*

# MONROE

Monroe walked into Grace's Diner nearly a month after Colt left. She had scoured the paper, searching for anything that could compare to her old job, but nothing did. She had taken a leap of faith when she saw this opening, it was nothing at all like what she wanted, but that didn't seem to matter too much at the moment. She had to find something. Anything. She refused to take money from her husband but without it she was sure to be delinquent on several bills soon. There was only so much she could do without to make ends meet.

An older woman stood behind a wooden counter, pencil behind her ear. She pushed a strand of white hair out of her eyes and smiled, looking across the room at Monroe.

"Hey honey, sit anywhere you'd like. I'll follow you."

Monroe shook her head, approaching the bar quickly. "Actually, I'm not here to eat. I'm looking for the owner."

The woman put her pad of paper down, staring at her. "Well, you found her. What can I do for you?"

Monroe swallowed hard, sticking out her hand, shaking

the woman's firmly. "I'm here about the job you have posted in the paper."

A smile filled the woman's wrinkled face. "Oh, great! I'm Grace."

"Monroe," Monroe introduced herself.

"Well, Monroe, what experience do you have?"

"Well," she said hesitantly. "None. I've been in an office for the past thirty years nearly. Up until last week." She paused. "It's kind of a long story. But, look, I'm a fast learner and a hard worker. Just tell me what to do and put me to work."

The woman gave her an odd look. After a moment, she spoke. "If you don't mind me asking, what would make you want to come into waitressing after having worked in an office? They're entirely different worlds."

Monroe did, in fact, mind her asking. She sighed, expecting the question though hoping it wouldn't be asked. "My husband, soon to be ex-husband, was my boss. Now, I promise that won't interfere with my job performance—the divorce, I mean. But I just desperately need something else. And fast. I'll work weekends, holidays, whatever you need. I don't have any scheduling conflicts. No kids to get sick and cause me to miss work. If it doesn't work out, you can let me go, but I promise you won't regret giving me a chance."

The woman stared at her with a sour look on her face. Monroe was sure she was going to laugh her out of the building. After a moment, a small smile formed.

"My ex-husband was an ass too." She laughed. "When can you start?"

# MONROE

The phone rang as soon as she opened her front door, a load of groceries balancing delicately in her arms. She nearly dropped the bags in an attempt to rush into the room and shut the door before getting to the phone. She set them down, pulling the plastic straps off of her arms in a hurry. She ignored the clanging noise as they bumped together, no doubt breaking something, and ripped open her purse. The bags had left red and white lines down the porcelain of her forearms, she rubbed them gently before looking down into her purse. Her phone's glow lit up the inside, making it easy for her to locate it immediately.

"Hello?" she called into the speaker, though it wasn't quite to her ear just yet.

"Hi." The voice on the other end of the line was quiet. Her heart immediately fell, it wasn't the person she'd been hoping to hear from. She ran a hand through her disheveled hair, trying to slow down her rapid breathing. "Is this, um, is this Monroe?"

"Yes, it is," Monroe answered, trying to decide whether she recognized the voice.

"Monroe, hello. It's Natalie Pearman from Pearman and Portman. I was calling because you'd missed your appointment again. I wanted to make sure that everything was all right and to see if you were planning to reschedule." She spoke with a soft uncertainty.

Monroe was still for a moment. "I'm sorry, that sounds familiar...my schedule has just been so crazy and chaotic lately. Can you remind me of what the job was? I've put in so many resumes lately I can't seem to keep track." She paused, realizing immediately how that must sound. "Oh, but please don't let that affect your hiring decision. This is so unlike me. I swear I'm usually very reliable."

"Oh no. I'm sorry, you misunderstood. This isn't about a job. I'm a psychologist with a practice called Pearman and Portman. You called me a few weeks ago to request an emergency appointment. When you missed it, we rescheduled for this week. Yesterday, in fact. I was a little concerned when you didn't show up again. You sounded upset when we spoke the last time."

Monroe racked her brain, trying to recall this woman or the appointment. The first days, weeks even, after Colt had left were a haze of alcohol and sleep deprivation. If she had called the woman, she probably sounded like a sobbing lunatic and she was embarrassed to say she couldn't remember the conversation at all.

Not wanting to admit to the stranger how bad her memories of those weeks were, she decided to fake it. "Oh, right. Well, listen, I'm honestly fine. My husband and I are going through a rough separation and I didn't deal with it well at first. I'm so much better now, though. Honestly, I am.

I won't be needing to schedule any further appointments but I am so sorry to have wasted your time."

"It's no waste, Monroe," the woman responded politely. "I was glad to be able to speak with you. I would really love the chance to meet you. If you'd let me, I believe it could really be beneficial to you. Divorce can be tough and sometimes talking through it with someone can help."

"You're very kind," Monroe said. "But I'm sure I'll be just fine. It's going to be rough time for a while but it's already so much better." Her eyes drifted to the two empty whiskey bottles on her counter with guilt.

"Monroe, it's great to hear that. Honestly, it really is. I would feel so much better though if you'd allow me to meet with you anyway. Just one half hour session even. Sometimes you don't realize how much you're hurting, how much you need someone to listen, until you are able to sit down and reflect."

Monroe shook her head, though the woman couldn't see it. She could feel her heart beating loudly in her chest and beads of sweat began to pool between her hand and the phone.

"Look," she said finally, "this is embarrassing. Even if I wanted to come in for a session, I couldn't afford it. My husband's income is gone now and I've only recently started a new job. I won't have enough money to pay you for several weeks, if ever. I have too many bills to catch up on as it is right now. I really appreciate your concern, but it's just not a good time for me to add any extra expenses to my life right now."

"I know that," the doctor responded without hesitation.

"You know that?"

"Yes. You mentioned it the last time we talked. We also

talked about how your husband will be paying for your sessions. I believe you said he was the one who suggested that you meet with me in the first place."

"Oh...right," Monroe mumbled. The memory was starting to come back to her now, hazy and dreamlike. There was no telling how much she'd had to drink that night. She may never have remembered the conversation at all, had the doctor not called.

"So, what do you say?" she asked, interrupting her thoughts. "Just one session?"

"Well, okay, I guess," Monroe answered. "But I should probably check with Colt first, just to be sure. I mean, since he's going to be paying for it."

"Oh, of course. Well, what does your schedule look like tomorrow? If everything checks out with him, obviously. I just had a last minute cancellation and I should be able to squeeze you in around two, if that works for you?"

"Tomorrow should be fine."

"Great. And two o'clock works? I could make it three if we need to."

"Two o'clock is fine," Monroe said, still trying to scrape the rest of the whiskey-coated memory from her skull.

---

WHEN MONROE PULLED into the driveway of the townhouse where Colt had begun staying, a lump rose in her throat. She studied the outside of his house, trying to decide if it looked happy, and subsequently if he was happy. She saw his maroon Honda sitting in the driveway, leaving just enough space for another car to fit. She tried to push the thought from her mind, but it was already there. *This was where Jenna's car would park.*

Monroe wondered if he'd already moved her in with him. It wouldn't totally surprise her. Maybe he was waiting, though, enjoying his new bachelor life. She stared at the house for a long time once she'd stopped the car, her skin tingling with anticipation and fear. Everything in her entire body wanted her to turn around and leave, her heart aching at knowing his home was no longer with her. That it would never be with her again. Still, she remained strong. She pushed the door open, climbing out of the car. The humid Mississippi air hit her with a vengeance. She brushed her fingers through her hair casually as she made her way up the small set of steps in front of the townhouse, willing herself to calm down. Her hair clung to her neck immediately, her body coated with sweat and she knew it was no use. She was a nervous wreck and her hair wasn't going to tame just by running her fingers through the tangles.

As she approached the large oak door and pressed the doorbell, her heart fluttered with a new emotion: hope. She hadn't seen Colt in the weeks since he'd left and it filled her with excitement at the mere possibility of seeing him again. She heard footsteps approaching the door from inside the house, running toward her. Was he running to see her? She listened closely. The footsteps sounded so small through the door.

Suddenly, the door swung open and with it, her heart sank. A little girl stood before her, her coal black curls flowing wildly as she swung open the door.

The word escaped her mouth, "Mommy!" though her face fell instantly when she realized it was Monroe waiting for her, rather than her mother. Following close behind, Colt touched the girl's shoulder gently, his eyes on Monroe.

"Go back to the living room, Tiff. Go play with your toys, okay?"

The girl nodded, turning around and running away. He then addressed Monroe, grief filling his tired eyes. He ran his hands through his dark hair in what Monroe realized must be frustration.

"Monroe? What are you doing here?"

"I—" She couldn't speak, her voice caught in her throat. "Who was that?"

He sighed, rubbing his forehead as he so often did when he was stressed. "Her name is Tiffany."

"Is she...is she yours? She's...I mean, how old? Is she? How could this—how old is she?" Her words came out in fragments, each breath more difficult than the last as she prayed she was wrong. Her chest grew tight and she immediately covered her mouth, unsure if she was going to pass out or throw up next.

"She's two," he said stiffly, stepping out of the door and shutting it behind him. "What do you want, Monroe?"

"Is she...I mean...who is...is she yours? Your daughter? Do you—" She spoke with a quiet breathlessness that sucked the life out of her sentences. How could she possibly make sense of her racing thoughts? Each word hurt her. Finally, she sucked in a deep breath, gathering her resolve. "Was that your daughter, Colt?"

He sighed, pressing his lips together and rubbing his chin in annoyance. He crossed his arms in front of him before speaking again. His face seemed to have aged so much since she'd seen him last, though she knew it couldn't be possible. "Yes, Monroe. Yes, I have a daughter."

His words hit her with a force she hadn't expected. Cool tears formed in her eyes. "Oh."

He stared at her in silence, waiting for a response. "Is she...is it Jenna? Jenna's daughter? You and Jenna?" Monroe spit out the words, hoping the tears wouldn't fall, yet she couldn't seem to stop them.

"Yes," he said softly. "Jenna is her mother."

She sucked in a breath, not fully prepared for that answer. "But we've only been separated for one month." Another tear fell down her cheek but she didn't dare move.

"I'm sorry, Monroe," he said, though his face showed no signs of being sorry.

*"You're sorry?"*

"Yes. I am. I didn't want you to...I didn't want to do this. Not this way."

"You're sorry?" she fumed at him, her voice rising in anger. "You're sorry? Are you serious? I don't even know who you are anymore, Colt. I thought you loved me. I thought we were happy. I thought you'd just...I don't know, made a mistake. But, clearly I was very wrong. You've had this whole other life, this other *family.* All this time? And now all you can say is that you're sorry? I don't understand. How can you do this? How can you do this to me, Colt? To me? To our marriage. Haven't I been good to you? What did I do to deserve this? What did she do? What's so...special about her?" She was asking the questions that had been in her mind for so long. The questions she wasn't sure she wanted the answers to as she interrogated him through her tears.

He placed his hand on her shoulder calmly. "Monroe, please just stop. I can't do this right now. Not here. Not like this." He exhaled through his nose. "Look, why are you even here? What are you doing? Do you need something? You know you shouldn't have come."

Monroe took a breath, looking around the quiet subdivision. Her pride kept her from the complete meltdown she could feel coming on. With a shattered heart, she changed the subject, wiping away her tears. "I came to ask about a therapist. One called me earlier. Pearman something. She said you offered to pay for me to see her."

"Yes. I did."

"Why? Why would I be the one who needs to talk to her?" she asked him. "I'm not the reason we're this way. This is you, Colt. It isn't me. It isn't my fault."

"Yes," he said simply, "it is. You should go, Monroe." With that, he walked back into the house and shut the door.

# MONROE

Monroe walked into the office of Pearman and Portman with a quiet, nagging frustration. She was unsure of why she had even agreed to come. She felt much better most days, though the revelation yesterday about Colt's child had set her back quite a bit. It was understandable, she reminded herself, after such a surprise. Her feelings were to be expected.

"Hello there." A woman greeted her at the door, her dark hair pulled back into a neat ponytail. She beamed at Monroe happily. "You must be Monroe." She held out her hand for Monroe to shake. "I'm Dr. Pearman, but you can call me Natalie. I'm so glad to meet you."

"Thanks." Monroe shook her hand briefly before pulling it back, she offered up a small smile. The doctor led her through a door to her far left, closing the door behind them.

The office was quaint, very southern, with antique furniture sitting everywhere.

"I'm glad you were able to make it in today," Natalie said. "Have a seat anywhere you'd like."

Monroe did as she was told, sitting on a surprisingly comfortable chair that gave her easy access to the door, should she need it. The doctor continued to smile warmly at her, picking up a small notepad and sitting down across from her. She stared at her for a few moments before speaking.

"So, Monroe, let's start with something simple. Tell me how you've been feeling."

*Simple.* Monroe had to work to hold in a laugh. "Oh, I've been okay," she answered automatically.

"Okay, that's good to hear." Natalie didn't miss a beat. "Tell me about what you've been doing."

"Well, I got a new job. I'm working at a place called Grace's Diner as a waitress. It's not the best, you know, but it's something for now. Something to help me get back on my feet."

"What did you do before?"

*Before.* The word stung Monroe. Before Colt. Before the separation. Before her life was torn apart. Before this. She realized then, from that moment on her life would be classified two ways: before Colt and after Colt. She cleared her throat. "I was a secretary at my husband's, uh...at Colt's, insurance agency."

"Is that where you two met?"

"Oh my. No. We've been married for years now. Before he ever got into insurance. We were both still in college, in fact. And then, he was at the insurance agency long before he brought me on. It was his idea. I was a homemaker for the first several years after we were married. It was what he wanted and so I let my degree go to waste. Then, his secretary left and he suggested I come work for him, just to get out of the house. So, I did."

"Did you like it there?"

Monroe shrugged, glancing out the window. "Sure. Everyone was nice. When your husband owns the place, that's part of it, I guess."

"So, when did you leave?"

Before she could answer, the air conditioning came on and the vent above her head blew straight down, causing her to shiver. She fidgeted with a piece of hair that kept blowing into her eyes. Finally, she stood up, moving to a more comfortable seat and rubbing her arms to warm them back up.

"I'm sorry, what did you ask?"

"That's all right," Natalie told her. "I asked when you decided to leave your husband's agency."

"Right. Well, after we separated, it just didn't seem right to stay. I basically only had the job because of my husband anyway. He wouldn't have wanted me to stay, but he's too polite to have ever said that. Besides, it would just be too hard on me to have to see him every day."

"I see. So, what caused your split?"

"He was having an affair," she said quickly, not looking at Natalie. "Apparently for a lot longer than I realized. Once I found out, I left. Or rather, I asked him to."

"Just like that? After all these years?"

Monroe's jaw dropped open. "Well, yes. There's no amount of time that would keep me in a marriage like that. I won't sit around and let my husband cheat on me. I'm not that girl. I would never forgive myself if I let him come back home."

"Even if you loved him?"

"Even *though* I love him," Monroe said defensively.

"So, when did you last speak to or see your husband?"

"Yesterday, actually. After our talk, I went to make sure he was still okay with paying for my sessions."

"And he was?"

"Well, obviously." Monroe frowned at her.

Natalie leaned forward over her notepad, her brow furrowed. "Monroe, I understand this is difficult for you. I appreciate your time so much, but I can sense that you're feeling hostile. Can I ask why that is?"

Monroe sighed. "I'm sorry. I know you're trying to help. It's just...it's all just too much."

"All?" Natalie sat back in her chair, her pen scribbling along the lines. Monroe wondered what she could be writing.

"Yes, all. This. This session. The divorce. Finding and starting a new job, a new life. My husband's secret family. I just can't handle it. I'm too old for all this change." Emotions she hadn't allowed herself to feel burst out of her.

Natalie nodded. "This is certainly a trying time, even for the strongest person. Tell me, how are you dealing with it all? What's your coping mechanism?"

"I'm just...dealing. I mean, I wake up, go to work, come home, and go to bed. I don't want to deal with it. I just want to wake up and realize this has all been some bad dream. But it's not."

"No." Natalie shook her head. "No, Monroe. It's not just a bad dream."

---

MONROE LEFT the diner at half past three, her arm still burning from carrying so many hot plates throughout the day. Her entire body reeked of greasy, fried food. She wore the smell home with her daily now. It stuck to her clothes no matter how much she washed them.

She hurried down the busy sidewalk, zigzagging in between people, headed for Natalie's office. She glanced at her watch without checking the time. It was pointless. She was already late. Her thoughts traveled back to the diner, wondering if she'd remembered to collect her tip from the last table. Keegan was her busboy and the rumors were that he liked to collect tips and report them as less than they actually were. She usually made sure to check, but the day had run over and she'd completely forgotten. She sighed, walking into Natalie's building.

Today, there was one other person waiting, which surprised her. Natalie's office had been fairly quiet every time she'd been in so far. The woman smiled at her politely and looked away.

Monroe did the same. After a few awkward minutes, the door swung open and Natalie walked out into the lobby, a young girl following close behind her.

"We had a really great session today, Mrs. Meyer. Chelsey did a great job." She smiled politely at the woman on the couch, who stood up to greet the girl.

"Thanks, Natalie. How are you feeling, Chels?"

"Fine, Mom." The irritated preteen groaned as she pushed her mother's arms away.

The woman smiled awkwardly at Natalie. "Thanks again. We'll see you next week. Tell her good-bye, Chelsey," she coaxed.

The girl threw an angry hand over her shoulder in an agitated wave as she shoved the door open, her worried mother following close behind.

"I'm sorry you had to see that." Natalie turned to address Monroe, a half-grin on her face.

"Eh, we were all bitchy teens at some point, right?" Monroe shook her head in laughter.

Natalie nodded, looking relieved. "That's what I hear."

She held her hand up, leading Monroe further into her office and through the door to where their sessions took place. They took their usual seats and Natalie began just as she always did.

"So, how are you feeling today, Monroe?"

"I'm all right." Monroe looked down at her arm, where the redness was starting to form a blister. "I burned my arm on a hot plate at work, so that's annoying, but what can you do?"

Natalie frowned at her. "You know that's not exactly what I meant." Monroe knew, but she didn't bother to respond. When she realized Monroe wasn't going to elaborate, Natalie continued. "All right, well, I guess we'll just jump right in then. Have you spoken to Colt?"

"Not since I found out about his daughter, no. I don't plan to."

"I can certainly understand why you'd feel that way. Do you think you would consider at least speaking to him long enough to give him a chance to explain?"

Monroe shook her head. "No, I don't think so. He has a two-year-old daughter and we separated less than two months ago. I don't need any further explanation. He's a cheater and a liar and that's not the man I agreed to spend my life with. I thought he was someone different, someone I could trust. Why is it you seem to be on his side, anyway?"

"There are no sides, Monroe. And I wouldn't be on anyone's side even if there were. I'm trying to take care of you. I just want you to have peace with everything that's happened."

"I'll never make peace with this, Natalie. Never. He told me he didn't want kids. Not then. Not yet. He always said we weren't ready. That's why we never had them. Now, I'm old and barren and he's out there being a father to someone else's child. I gave thirty years of my life to that man and he just threw it all away." Monroe exploded at Natalie, releasing her anger, as she usually did at some point during their sessions.

Natalie didn't budge, her face calm, as she waited for Monroe to finish. "Monroe, do you worry he didn't want children with you, rather than at all?"

"Of course I do. Of course. He always seemed so set on it. Then one day, we're fifty years old and his 'not yet' became our 'never'."

"But you wanted children?" She squinted her eyes at her, trying to understand.

Monroe pondered the question, letting the answer sit on her tongue. *Yes.* Yes, she had wanted children. She'd always wanted them. "I would've been a horrible parent," she admitted, rubbing her temple. She stood, needing to catch her breath, and walked to the window, watching the trees blow in the heavy wind.

"Oh? Why do you say that?" she asked politely.

"I had a horrible role model." Monroe laughed through her pain.

"What do you mean? Did you have a rough relationship with your mother?"

"I never had a mother," Monroe said with a scoff. "I had dozens. I was in and out of foster care my whole life. Left behind and forgotten about. I was put into my first home before I can even remember and transferred around until I turned seventeen. Then, when I could, I just walked away from it all. The second that I could."

"So, you never knew either of your biological parents?"

"Nope." She choked back tears, hoping Natalie wouldn't notice them. "Didn't want to."

"What about siblings? Did you have any that you know of?"

"Sure. I had a ton of foster siblings. Kids like me, who no one really cared about. But I was never anywhere for long enough to get to know any of them. I was never anywhere for more than a few months." She paused. "Well, I guess that's not entirely true, the last home I was at I stayed for close to a year, I think. It's too far back to even remember now."

"Did you get along with your foster families? Were they kind to you?"

"Look," Monroe said, turning to face her abruptly. "I don't mean to be rude but what does any of this have to do with anything? It's all done. Over with. It happened so long ago. It has nothing to do with what's going on now."

"I don't think that's true, Monroe. Every part of your past affects you now. Maybe more than you realize."

"I didn't get along with them, then. Is that what you want to hear?" She walked back over to the couch and flopped down angrily. "Does that give you the magical answer to saving me?"

"I want to hear the truth." Natalie nodded, encouraging her to continue. Her voice was as calm as possible considering Monroe's outburst.

"The truth? The truth is that none of it matters now. None of it matters because the one person who actually cared is gone now. And I don't know why. I don't know what

I did to make him leave me, to make him cheat. He always seemed so happy. And I just keep wondering, you know, did I miss it? Did I miss how unhappy he was? Were there signs? Was I so busy with my own stupid happiness that I just didn't see the truth?" She let out a sudden sob she hadn't been expecting. "I really loved him, Natalie. Love. Loved. It's all such a blur now. I never, *never,* expected it to go like this. Our marriage was perfect to me. I know people say no marriage is perfect, but ours was pretty close. At least I thought so. Until that night. Until it wasn't."

Natalie looked at her with a troubled expression, begging her to continue.

# MONROE

Monroe looked around the room, a glass of chilled vodka cooling her hand. She'd been sobbing loudly every few minutes since she left Natalie's office. It was *such a breakthrough,* Natalie had said, that she had been able to talk about the things she had refused to for so long. *So healthy for her.*

Monroe felt anything but healthy though, as she sat crying in her all too quiet house. It was as if, overnight, everything in her life had fallen apart. She'd been left all alone to pick up and discard the pieces of what she'd believed would last forever.

There is a kind of sadness that no one talks about. The sadness that sits on a deep, dark spectrum of depression. Monroe had felt it growing in her soul for most of her life, eating away at her sanity, stripping away every piece of happiness she'd ever had. She'd fought back daily. Some days it took all of her effort just to get out of bed. Some days the sadness was a distant memory. In the days since Colt had left, keeping the sadness at bay was nearly impossible. The darkness had no name and she never knew when to expect it, only that she could see it coming in the days that it grew close. Swarming her head like black bumblebees, the sadness could be seen, causing her migraine to swell to an enormity she'd only known during these times. The past hurt her to this day, physically and mentally, it was all too much. Every time she opened up and let it out, this was her punishment.

She took a gulp of her drink, its warmth filling her chest. Another sob escaped her mouth and she let herself slide further down into the leather couch, her skin sticking and groaning with her every move. A knock on her door sounded, startling her. She sat up, sloshing vodka down her shirt. She lazily attempted to mop up a small amount that hit the couch with her blanket and then stood up, making her way to the door slowly.

"Who is it?" she called.

"Open the door, Monroe." His voice hit her hard, causing her jaw to drop and her breath to catch in her chest. Was she imagining him?

"C-Colt?" she stammered, headed toward the door in what felt like slow motion. Her whole world spun.

"Yes, it's me," he called through the door. "Let me in please."

She swung the large wooden door open quickly, staring at her husband in disbelief. "What are you doing here?" she asked.

"Are you drunk?" he asked with a scowl, his voice drenched in frustration.

"What are you doing here, Colt?" she asked again. He pulled open the glass screen door, stepping into the condo without permission. She took a step back, nearly tripping over her own feet. He caught her arm in an attempt to stop her from crashing to the ground. Both of their faces turned red as their skin met. She pulled her arm away quickly, looking down. "You shouldn't be here," she told him, avoiding his eye contact. She moved her hand to where his palm had been on her arm, wanting desperately to feel his touch again.

"I know," he admitted.

"So, then why are you?" She looked up at him finally, her voice wavering.

"I missed you," he said simply, his eyes locked with hers.

She pulled her gaze away. "That's not enough," she told him firmly.

"I know," he said and then, before she could comprehend what was happening, he was kissing her. His lips locked with hers, carrying a fierce passion she'd missed for so long. She threw her arms around his neck, lifting her legs to grip his back. He picked her up with ease, carrying her to the kitchen. His strong arms surrounded her body, making her feel safe as they always had. He laid her on the dining room table, not bothering to pull their lips apart even once. His beard burned her chin in an all too familiar way. His breath smelled of coffee and mint gum, a combination she'd grown to miss.

It seemed impossible to her how much she'd missed this man, how much she loved this man. In that very moment, nothing else mattered: not the affair, not his daughter, not all of the lies, nothing. She just wanted to be with him. To be loved by him again.

Their kisses stopped abruptly. Monroe was unsure who had actually stopped first. She made herself breathe deep, trying desperately to catch her breath. She panted, clutching her chest, and placed one arm behind her on the table to prop herself up.

"What does this mean, Colt?" she asked, not sure she wanted to know the answer.

"What?" he asked, staring at her in confusion, his face only inches from hers.

"Did you," she paused, almost afraid to ask. "Did you leave Jenna?"

He frowned. "Can we please just not go there? Please? Not now. Not tonight. Just kiss me. Please just...just kiss me." He leaned into her, holding her face to his, begging for another kiss.

She pushed him away with force, jumping down from the table. "No. I can't. I can't just pretend that everything is okay. You have to tell me. Tell me that you left her. Tell me that it's over between you two, Colt."

He stared at her, his eyes filled with a wild grief. Finally, he shook his head. "You didn't leave her?" she asked, confirming what she already assumed. Again, his head shook.

She nodded, looking away as tears filled her eyes. She looked back toward him, forcing him to watch as the tears he'd created fell. "Do you still love her?"

"Please don't," he said softly, reaching his hand for hers.

She stayed still, their skin only inches from each other. "Answer me. Do you still love Jenna, Colt?"

"Yes," he said finally. "Yes. I do. I will always love Jenna."

More tears filled her eyes as the shred of happiness she'd held onto diminished. She pushed him back further, turning to walk toward the front door.

"You should go," she said through her tears.

"Please don't do this," he called from behind her. "Please. I need to be with you tonight. I just need you. We had a life together. That doesn't just go away. I can't walk away from you like nothing mattered. Not after everything we've been through together. Not after all this time."

"You already did, Colt." She choked back tears as alcohol, rage, and utter heartbreak fought for their place inside of her cloudy mind. Her emotions shut down as she pulled open the door, pointing him to his exit. "You already did."

# MONROE

Monroe squeezed her eyes shut and opened them again, trying to shake the memory of the previous night. The small coffee shop bustled with patrons on the busy Monday afternoon. At a booth across from her, a gentleman caught her eye, tipping his gray mug toward her and smiling.

He was dressed in a business suit, his red tie standing out nicely against the black of his jacket. She smiled back at him politely, wondering if she knew him. He didn't seem familiar, but then again, lately her memory wasn't to be relied on. He took a sip of his coffee, looking away. Monroe did the same, forgetting that hers was still too hot and jumping as it scalded her mouth.

She cursed loudly as the hot coffee ran down her blouse, scorching her skin. Instantly, the man was at her side, handing her a napkin. She took it gratefully, stuffing it down her shirt. She was sure she was giving him quite an eyeful as she pulled her shirt away from her chest, but she was in too much pain to care.

He sat down across from her. "You okay, sweetheart? That looked painful."

Once the coffee had been wiped up and her skin cooled down, she stood up. "I'm fine, thank you. I should go though. Coffee stains don't really go with this outfit." She tried to laugh, though embarrassment filled her.

He stood up next to her, chuckling. "On the contrary, I think it looks very nice."

She stopped then, really noticing him for the first time. He was a handsome man, maybe a few years older than Colt. He stood quite a bit taller than her, a head full of thick, gray hair. She smiled at him, welcoming the attention she'd been craving since Colt had walked out. Her husband wasn't the only one who could find someone else, she reminded herself. "Would you like to walk me home?" she asked him.

His eyes grew wide. He seemed to think about the proposition for a moment before answering. "Well, sure. I suppose I could. What side of town do you live on?"

"I'm at the town line, almost to Portland. It's sort of a long walk," she warned him. "But, it's a nice day."

"What? You don't think an old geezer like me can make it?" He winked at her.

She smirked up at him. "Care to prove me wrong?"

He held out his hand, taking hers gently. "I'm Harrison."

"Hi, Harrison. I'm Monroe," she told him, feeling her face grow warm. They made their way out the door and down the street before he spoke again.

"So, what do you do, Monroe?"

"Right now I'm a waitress," she told him. "At Grace's Diner." She pointed in the general direction of the diner and he nodded, though he didn't mention if he knew the place.

"Well, maybe I could come see you there sometime."

"I'd like that." She smiled at him flirtatiously. He placed an arm around her waist, giving her butterflies like she hadn't felt in years. Her face burned as she began to blush again. As they continued walking, she received several peculiar looks from passersby, staring at the coffee stain down the front of her shirt. She crossed her arms in front of herself, wishing they'd all stop staring. She'd never liked having people notice her. Except Colt. The day they met, Colt told her he couldn't keep his eyes off of her. That made her feel good. Beautiful. People as handsome as he was didn't often notice plain girls like her.

She shook her head, looking at Harrison and trying to listen as he spoke. Colt had no place in her mind or life anymore. She had to remember that.

As the walk continued, she learned that Harrison owned a very successful investment firm in Biloxi and that he was only in town for a few weeks on business. He told her about his children, two boys and a girl, and one brand new grandson. It made Monroe sad, listening to him talk, as she began to think of the life she and Colt could've had, had things been different.

Harrison told her he had two dogs: Mae and Misses. His wife had passed away three years before and he hadn't dated much since then. Monroe told him about the separation, about Colt, and about Jenna. She told him about their daughter. She tried very hard to keep the pain out of her voice as she spoke of her greatest heartbreak.

Harrison was a very good listener. He nodded in all of the right places and chimed in when she needed him to. When they got back to her condo, Monroe opened the door without hesitation. He stopped walking, releasing his hand from her waist.

"Well," he said, kissing her hand. "I should go."

"You don't want to come inside?" Monroe asked, cocking her head to the side.

"Oh, I want to," he paused, his face growing red. "But I really shouldn't. It wouldn't be right."

"Why not?" she asked, nearly offended.

"I mean, you know, just meeting you and all. It doesn't seem very good. On my part. Why, a pretty, young thing like you, I'm sure you have men all over you. If I go in, well, to be honest, I'm not sure I'd be able to leave." He was fumbling his words, obviously embarrassed.

Monroe stared at him for a moment, watching his expression. Colt hadn't had to be asked twice on their first date. He'd just gone for it. She'd take a page from his book, she decided, and make the first move. She pushed herself up on her tiptoes, wrapping her arms around Harrison's neck and kissed him firmly on the lips. He froze for a second before giving in and kissing her back. His kiss felt all wrong—sloppy and strange—but she ignored it. She'd never have a kiss she was used to if she didn't try to kiss someone new. She twisted the door handle, attempting to pull him inside, when suddenly she heard a voice in the distance calling her name. "Monroe!"

She jerked away from him, pushing him back, and staring out into the driveway. Natalie stood by her car, one hand on her brow to shield her eyes from the sun.

"Natalie?" she called out to her. "What are you doing here?"

Beside her, Harrison was breathing heavily. As Natalie grew closer, he nodded to her formally before addressing Monroe. "Well, I should get going."

Monroe sighed, too exhausted to argue with him, and

waved to him. Natalie made her way up the stairs, eyebrows raised. She didn't bother hiding her shocked expression as she passed Harrison. "What are you doing?" Monroe asked again.

"You skipped the last two sessions, Monroe. I came to check on you."

"Well, perfect timing," she said with a scoff.

"I can see that," Natalie said sarcastically, seemingly annoyed. "Who was that?"

"His name is Harrison," Monroe said defensively. She pushed open the door, allowing Natalie to walk past her and into the house.

"Is he your boyfriend? I don't believe you've mentioned him before, in your sessions." She glanced over her shoulder where Harrison could be seen walking down the street.

"I haven't. That's because I *don't believe* that's any of your business. I didn't ask you to come check on me, Natalie. It isn't your place. I'm a grown woman and I can do what I want. I've been taking care of myself and making my own decisions for a very long time, believe it or not. Longer than you've been alive, in fact."

"Of course you have. I'm sorry, Monroe. I didn't mean to overstep here. I wasn't asking as your therapist, but rather as your friend."

"My friend? My husband is paying you to talk to me for an hour a week. That doesn't leave much room for friendship." She set her purse down on the counter, walking to the bedroom and shutting the door.

"Well, sure it does," Natalie called from the living room. "I can be your friend, too." Monroe rolled her eyes, pulling a clean shirt over her head and tossing the dirty one into the hamper before exiting the bedroom. Natalie was standing in front of the entertainment center, staring at a picture of Monroe and Colt from vacation a few years back.

"You guys look so happy here," she said softly, running her fingers across the dusty frame.

"Yeah," Monroe agreed. "Well, we used to be happy."

"My husband and I went to this beach last year." She pointed to the picture of the two of them at Ormond Beach. "Florida beaches are so much different than ours, huh?" She pulled out her phone, not really looking for an answer. "I think I have a picture of us there." She scrolled through her phone, biting her bottom lip. "Yes, here." She held it out. Monroe stared at the screen briefly. In the photo, Natalie was standing on the shore next to a sign welcoming them to Ormond Beach, the same sign that she and Colt had stood next to for their own picture. Natalie wore a bright blue swimsuit, her arms wrapped casually around a man's waist. The man, her husband, was at least a half foot taller than her, his bushy dark blond hair looking windswept. Their smiles looked happy and carefree. It could've been a photo from a magazine. Monroe looked away, attempting to smile, though she couldn't summon a genuine one.

"I have other pictures too." She smiled, turning her phone back toward her. "Let's see, here's my daughter, Dawn. She just loves the beach, takes after me. We're both water babies. Her father couldn't care less." She showed Monroe a picture of a little girl, her dark hair curled neatly above her shoulders.

"She's beautiful," Monroe said honestly. *Just like her parents. Her perfect, happy parents.*

"Thank you." Natalie looked taken aback by the compliment.

"You're welcome. Now, what else can I do for you?"

Natalie put her phone away, her face suddenly serious. "You can tell me why you're skipping our sessions." She crossed her arms over her chest.

"Because I think I'm done coming," Monroe said, though she hadn't decided that until right then.

"What? Why? I thought we were really finding a good place in our time together."

"Yeah, Natalie, you keep saying that, but I don't really see it. Besides, I only agreed to one session and you got several more than that. I'm just done. I'm fine now. You've done your job."

"Have you forgiven him?" she asked stubbornly.

"What?"

"Because unless you've forgiven him, I haven't done my job. You'll still be struggling with this. You might not realize it now, but you'll struggle with your decision every day. You can't move on. It all comes down to accepting what has happened and finding the strength to forgive him. You don't have to like him, Monroe, but it's important that you forgive him. If not for him, for yourself."

"I'm sorry," Monroe said, anger filling her, "but who are you to tell me that? I will forgive my husband if and when I'm ready."

"Ex-husband," Natalie corrected.

"Ex-husband." Monroe nodded. "Husband until we sign the divorce papers."

"Are you ready to do that?" Natalie asked.

Monroe took a step back, wagging her finger in the air. "Don't try to shrink me. I'm not paying for this. We didn't have a session today. I'm done. Out. I'm sorry. Thank you for trying to help but I just can't do it anymore."

"Okay," Natalie agreed.

"Okay?"

"I don't agree with your decision but I certainly can't force you to attend sessions."

Monroe held her arm out, gesturing toward the door. "Okay. So, if there's nothing else?"

"Right." Natalie pressed her lips together in obvious frustration at her defeat. "I'll be going."

Monroe followed her toward the door.

"By the way," Natalie said, stopping and turning to face Monroe one last time. "Whose baby was that? In the picture of you and your husband at the beach?"

"Baby?" Monroe asked. "There's no baby in that picture." Natalie stared at her strangely. "There's no baby," Monroe insisted. She'd seen the picture a thousand times, she knew what she was talking about. She wouldn't allow Natalie to find another reason to delay her leaving.

Natalie shrugged. "I could've sworn there was. I'll see you around, Monroe. Take care of yourself." Monroe shut the door as Natalie walked away from it and down the porch steps. She turned around, curiosity looming in her, and walked back toward the entertainment center. She approached the photo, staring at it in the dim afternoon light. She was there, smiling in her bright white dress, her black hair flowing in the wind. Beside her, Colt stood, his swim trunks hugging his golden brown skin. She looked closer, as if it were a new picture, and gasped. In her arms was a white blanket, wrapped around a small, red faced baby. She took a deep breath, squinting her eyes, trying to figure out how it was possible, what sort of joke this must be, and then it all went black.

# MONROE

Monroe sat in the restaurant across from Harrison. She stared at his yellow bow tie, a tad crooked, and thought about reaching across the table and adjusting it. Instead, she remained still, a stiff smile on her face.

"I'm so glad we ran into each other again," he told her warmly, interrupting her thoughts.

She adjusted the strap of her black dress, nodding in agreement. "This time I didn't even have to pour coffee all over myself to get you to talk to me."

He chuckled at her. "No, you certainly didn't have to do that."

"So, how has your day been?" she asked him, making small talk while their waitress wandered around aimlessly. She searched the crowd, ignoring whatever answer he gave, hoping to see their drinks headed toward them. It had been nearly thirty minutes since they'd ordered and though the restaurant was busy, she was starting to grow impatient. Across from her, she heard Harrison fall suddenly silent and then there was an 'Uh-oh.'

"Uh-oh?" She snapped her attention to him. "Uh-oh what?"

He pointed behind her, toward the door. She turned, wondering what to expect and groaned as she saw Natalie walking into the restaurant. She had her dark hair tossed up into a loose ponytail and a bright red dress on. It was the first time Monroe had seen her dressed up and she realized quickly how stunning she was. She made a beeline straight for Monroe's table, an exuberant smile on her face.

"Hello! Imagine running into you two here," Natalie exclaimed. Without skipping a beat she turned to Harrison. "I don't think we've officially met yet," she told him, holding out her hand. "I'm Natalie, a friend of Monroe's."

Harrison, looking overwhelmingly sheepish, held out his hand as well. "I'm Harrison. It's nice to officially meet you."

"Oh," Natalie said, as she reached behind her, grabbing a man's arm as he approached the table. Monroe hadn't noticed him headed their way. "This is my husband, Dustin."

Dustin smiled at them both, holding out his hand. He had thick, dark blond hair that stood up on top of his head. His deeply tanned complexion stood out against Natalie's pale skin. They looked beautiful together, though Monroe couldn't help but notice that Natalie's body had gone stiff with him beside her.

"Hello," Monroe told him quietly. "I'm Monroe."

"It's nice to finally meet the famous Monroe." She smiled at him, though she was instantly overcome by a state of uneasiness. Something about Dustin made her feel on edge. What did he know about her? What had Natalie shared? She wanted them to leave, her eyes pulled away from them, focusing on a dirty spot on her menu. She flicked a crumb off the table.

"Oh, wow. Do you guys mind if we join your date?" Dustin asked. "This place is packed."

"Dustin!" Natalie scolded.

"What?" He laughed. "They don't mind, honey." He looked straight to Monroe. "Do you?"

"Um," Monroe thought out loud, trying to decide on an excuse. "Well—"

"It's fine with me," Harrison assured her, reaching across the table and touching her hand lightly.

"See, then it's settled," Dustin announced, taking the seat beside her. Natalie looked uneasy but sat down as well.

"Okay, so what's good here? Can you believe we've never been to this place? Natalie always tried to convince me to try it but, I don't know, it feels a little stuck up, don't you think?" Dustin asked, his gaze burning into her as he rambled.

Monroe looked down, wanting desperately to get out of the situation. Nothing felt right. Every hair on her arms stood at attention as he grazed the menu next to her, blissfully unaware of how uncomfortable she was. She could smell his cologne, its overpowering metallic scent made her stomach churn. All of the sudden, she felt very dizzy. She stood up, bumping the table and causing their menus to go flying.

"Monroe?" Natalie called out, staring at her in shock.

"Monroe, what is it?" Harrison asked. She made a move to get past them, unable to say a word. She tried to catch her breath as she exited the restaurant, coughing loudly as sobs escaped her chest.

"Monroe?" She heard a voice from behind her, felt hands on her back, but she couldn't answer. Couldn't turn around. She sank to the ground, feeling the cool, wet pavement on her bare legs. Her chest felt tight, each breath harder to take than the last. She gasped for air over and over, clutching her throat. What was happening to her? Her whole body shook as she rocked back and forth on the ground, closing her eyes tighter and tighter. The whole world seemed too small for her at the moment, the people and cars passing by making her feel claustrophobic.

"She's having a panic attack," she heard Natalie tell someone. "Give her some space."

The hands immediately left her back and she was alone. Then, there was that smell again. His awful cologne. A scream ripped from her throat and the world around her grew fuzzy as she slipped away from consciousness and faded into black.

# MONROE

Monroe opened her eyes and took a deep breath. The world around her was dark. In the distance, she could see a small amount of light creeping in from under the closet door. *Why am I in the closet?* Her memory was hazy from the previous day. She only remembered running into Harrison at the coffee shop again. Had she gotten drunk? Her head felt heavy, her mouth dry, much like a hangover.

She sat up, the rough carpet scraping her skin. Her memory was a completely blank slate. She hadn't been so hungover in ages.

She pushed open the closet door, covering her eyes as the bright light from her window blinded her. She crawled across the bedroom floor, her head pounding, and stood up finally in her doorway. Her body felt wobbly and weak. She made her way into the kitchen, grabbing a glass of room temperature water and gulping it as if it were nectar from the gods.

"Glad to see you finally woke up." A unexpected voice from behind her startled her, causing her to throw her water, the glass shattering at her feet. She turned around, staring in shock.

"What are you doing here?" she demanded.

Natalie bent to pick up the shattered glass. "I was worried about you. I stayed to make sure you were okay."

"I'm fine," Monroe told her, bending to pick up the glass as well. A sharp piece cut her hand, sending a trail of blood down her arm. She cursed loudly, slapping her other hand over the wound.

*"Oh no, Monroe.* Here." Natalie stood up, trying to help. She grabbed a handful of paper towels, handing them over.

"Thanks," Monroe mumbled. "Thanks for staying too, you didn't have to."

"I know that." Natalie nodded, turning on the faucet so that Monroe could rinse her hand.

"I guess I just had too much to drink last night. I can't hold my alcohol like I used to. You just wait. Enjoy your youth while you've got it," she joked.

Natalie shook her head, her face filled with confusion. "You don't remember what happened?"

"What?" Monroe asked over the noise of the faucet, the water stinging her cut.

Natalie spoke slowly when she responded. "Monroe, you hadn't been drinking. You aren't hungover. And it wasn't last night."

"What are you talking about?" She shut off the water, holding the towels on her wound, watching the white material turn red.

"You've been sleeping for two straight days. I've tried to wake you up several times but you just wouldn't wake." Monroe stared up at her in disbelief, the cut on her hand suddenly forgotten. "You hadn't been drinking, Monroe. Not even close. You hadn't gotten so much as a glass of water when Dustin and I arrived at the restaurant."

"Dustin?" Monroe asked, feeling lost.

Natalie pursed her lips. "You had a panic attack two nights ago. A bad one. Has that ever happened to you before?"

"What are you talking about?"

Natalie touched her hand, her voice in full-on shrink mode. "What's the last thing you remember clearly?"

Her head pounded as she tried to think back over the black shadow that clouded her mind. "I, um, I don't know." She bit her lip as she tried to remember. Something. Anything. It was as if her mind was completely empty. Blank. She couldn't remember a single thing. "Colt and Harrison." Her eyes filled with tears as, finally, a memory came to her. "I remember Harrison."

"Okay," Natalie said calmly. "Let's sit down." She put an arm around Monroe's shoulder as she ushered her over to the kitchen table. Monroe allowed it to happen, her world feeling eerie around her.

"Okay," Monroe said as she sat down.

"Okay," Natalie repeated. "So, you remember Harrison?" She nodded, coaxing the words out of Monroe.

"Yes." She scrunched her brow, trying to recall the memory. "I remember going to the coffee shop. I ran into him there and...I remember that he asked me to dinner. I said I would go."

"Very good, Monroe. Do you remember going to dinner with him?"

"No," Monroe said firmly. "No. I never went."

Natalie raised her eyebrows, making Monroe frown. "Did I?"

Natalie was silent, staring at her patient. When she finally spoke, her voice was slow and steady. "Monroe, has this happened before? Panic attacks? Blacking out? Losing pieces of time?"

Monroe frowned again, shaking her head. "*No!* Of course not. I mean, I don't think so. How would I even know? Would I even know?"

To that, Natalie seemed to have no answer. "If we could figure out if it has happened before, maybe we could decipher what caused it." She looked at her as if she wanted her to say yes, that it had happened, but Monroe couldn't. She couldn't say this had happened before, but then again...she couldn't say it hadn't.

She sat silently, staring at Natalie. Still, there was nothing in her head that could explain the past night's events. Nothing made sense. Everything around her felt like a dream.

"Okay," Natalie said finally. "Well, that's okay. I have to go into the office soon anyway. I have another client this afternoon. But, when we have a little bit of time, I'd like to continue this conversation. I think it's really important that we try and figure out exactly what your mind is up to, Monroe. Not only for your happiness, but for your safety as well. Blacking out could be very dangerous. Would that be okay?"

Monroe thought for a moment. "Sure, I guess. But not today, okay? I appreciate you staying with me, but I just can't do this today. I'm really tired."

"That's fine," Natalie told her. "How about tomorrow, then? You should probably stay inside today anyway. Eat and rest. You haven't had any food or water in two days. You need to make sure you, at the very least, hydrate."

Monroe agreed, standing up from the table. "Okay. I will. Tomorrow will work."

Natalie followed her toward the door, stopping briefly on her way out. She touched Monroe's hand lightly. "You'll take care of yourself, right?"

Monroe forced a smile. "I'll be fine, Natalie. I promise. But, thanks."

With that, she was gone, leaving Monroe alone with her strangely empty thoughts.

# MONROE

Monroe awoke on the couch. She immediately sat up, checking her memory. Was it still there? Could she still remember? Her headache was raging but from what she could tell, her memory was intact. No more dark clouds. *Natalie. The broken cup. The blood from her hand.* She looked down: the cut was fresh. She remembered the not remembering too, her mind still fresh with fear about what it could mean.

There was a knock on her door and she realized that was what had woken her up to begin with. Someone was there. She stood from the couch, making her way toward the door. *Natalie shouldn't have bothered coming back. Not so late anyway.* She glanced at the clock on the wall which showed it was just after eleven. It was too late for company.

She swung the door open, going to scold her therapist but stopped short. A man she didn't recognize stood in front of her. His shirt was only half buttoned, his ripped chest exposed. He smiled at her cockily. "Well, hey there."

"Who are you?" she asked, closing the door slightly.

Dread instantly began to creep over her. Her instincts told her this man was dangerous. Something wasn't right.

"You don't remember me?" he asked, feigning offense. "I'm shocked."

"I'm sorry, I think you have the wrong house," she told him firmly, attempting to shut the door. He stuck his arm out, catching the door and stopping her. As he did, she caught a gust of wind scented with his cologne. The scent was so strong her headache immediately intensified. "What the hell do you think you're doing?" she asked, trying to sound braver than she felt. Her knees shook beneath her and she hoped he wouldn't notice.

He smiled at her as if she may have been joking and the hairs on her arms stood up instantly, a sickly feeling washing over her.

"Monroe, isn't it?" he asked, her stomach knotting with ice cold fear as he said her name. She nodded, finding that her voice wouldn't work. "Well then, it's nice to meet you...again."

"Again?" she asked. "Who are you? You need to leave. My husband will be home any minute." Her voice was soft and unconvincing.

He laughed then, an outright chuckle. "You really don't remember me at all, do you? Do you even remember that your husband left?"

"How do you know—"

"I know a lot about you, Monroe. Almost everything there is to know, in fact."

"Like what?" The man moved closer to her, his cologne burning her nose. Her head spun, her breathing growing faster by the minute. "You should really go," she said again, standing her ground.

He reached his hand up, causing her to flinch in fear of what he may do, but he simply touched her cheek with the palm of his hand. His skin was rough against hers. "You're *so* beautiful," he whispered.

Her head and heart pounded in perfect rhythm and she pulled away from his touch. "Listen, I'm old enough to be your mother. Now, if you aren't going to tell me who you are or what you want, then leave." She spoke through gritted teeth, sounding braver than she felt. "Because I'm about ten seconds from calling the police."

He tutted his tongue playfully at her but finally turned to leave at her request, shaking his head as he went. "Good night, Monroe," he called over his shoulder. "I'll see you soon."

# MONROE

"Hello?" he whispered, his voice sounding groggy through the line.

"Colt?" she asked, her hands still shaking.

"Jenna?"

"No, it's Monroe," she said hastily, rubbing salt in her own wounds.

The worry in his voice depleted. "Oh. Monroe, what is it?"

"I, um, I was wondering if you could come over for a bit. I need your help," she told him.

"With what? *Jesus,* it's the middle of the night."

"I know," she said softly. She hated that she'd had to call him. She'd weighed all of her options before deciding this was her best. "But I really need you. Please."

He sighed, pausing for a moment. "All right, let me drop Tiffany off at my mom's house, okay? I'll be there in an hour."

"Thank you." She smiled to herself, feeling somewhat safer already.

---

WHEN HE SHOWED up an hour later, he was still dressed in his pajamas, his dark hair disheveled. He wore his old pair of glasses rather than the contacts she was used to.

"What's wrong?" he asked at the sight of her. She pulled her robe around her, shivering from the cool night air as she let him in.

"I'm okay." She waved off his concern.

"No, you aren't. You've been crying. What happened?" He walked closer toward her, his arms out, attempting to pull her into an embrace.

She backed up, fanning him away and holding out the package she'd bought. "Could you install an extra lock for me?"

He took the package from her hand, eyeing the deadbolt with a grave look on his face. "An extra lock? Monroe, what's going on?"

"Someone was here earlier." She choked out the sentence, fear overwhelming her again.

"Someone? What do you mean? Who?"

"A man," she told him. "I hope this works." She pointed to the lock. "I didn't know. I didn't want to go far or wait long. In case he was still around. It's all Benson's had. I know it's late but I couldn't sleep without it."

"Who was he? What did he look like?" Colt asked.

"I don't know, Colt. He didn't tell me his name. He...he knew me though, from somewhere. He was probably harmless, but it scared me a bit. I just want to be on the safe side. I wouldn't have called, it's just that I don't know that I could install it right. I wanted to make sure it was secure. I want to make sure that I'm safe. I'm really sorry. It was probably stupid."

"No, Monroe. You don't have to apologize." Colt's face was very serious, making her feel worse. "What did he do? Did he hurt you? What did he say?"

"He just seemed to know me really well. And more than what he said, it was the way he was looking at me. He just gave me a bad feeling, I can't explain it." Cold chills ran over her as she recalled the encounter. "I would just feel better having some extra protection."

"Okay," he said, "sure. Of course. I'm glad you called."

"Thank you, Colt. I know you don't have to do this kind of stuff for me anymore."

"Hey," he told her, staring at her. "I will always want you to be safe."

She nodded, turning her back to him and walking toward the kitchen. "Do you want some coffee? I'm going to make a pot for myself."

"Coffee would be great," he called to her. She walked to the counter, opening a cabinet and pulling out two mugs, filling them quickly. She put a teaspoon of sugar in hers, extra creamer in his. When she made it back to the living room, she handed over his mug, taking a sip of her own. "It has, uh, it's been a while since I've made coffee for two."

He nodded his head, putting the mug to his lips. "You still make a good cup."

"It's just coffee, Colt. There isn't much to it." She smiled at his compliment anyway.

"Well, thanks."

"You're welcome. It's the least I could do. Consider it an apology for the lack of sleep. I know it's late and, like I said, I know you don't have to do this stuff for me anymore. Or anything for that matter."

"Of course, Monroe. Like *I* said, I'm glad you called," he said seriously. "Just because we aren't together anymore doesn't mean I don't care about you."

"So, how are things?" She sat down on the couch, setting her mug on a coaster and pulling one out for him.

"Things are good." He set his mug down as well. She nodded, not sure what to say to the man she had so much to say to. *Where did Jenna think he was tonight? Did she know he was with her? Was she jealous? Should she be?* Thoughts raced through her mind. "So, I guess I should get to work," he said finally.

"Right." She pressed her lips together, nodding awkwardly. He opened the lock's packaging, pulling out the tools that it came with.

"Do you know how to install a lock?" she asked.

"Well, we both know I'm no handyman. But, it can't be too hard, right?" He smiled up at her. His smile was like a knife to the heart, so warm and familiar, yet a reminder of how much had changed. She spied the ring on his left hand, feeling shocked. *He still wore it.* She'd taken hers off weeks ago. Sheepishly, she covered her hand, wondering if he'd noticed yet. It was oddly comforting, seeing it there on his finger, in the place it had been for so many years. Then another, more cruel, thought entered her mind. *Would he someday wear a new ring? A ring for her?* She felt tears back in her eyes and stood suddenly, desperate to leave the room.

"You okay?" he asked her, watching her stand.

"I'm," she tried to answer him, but a sob caught in her throat and she closed her mouth, turning away from him.

With that, he was up and by her side in an instant. His

hands wrapped around her shoulders gently. "What is it? What's wrong?"

"I just, I miss you so much, Colt. I miss you every day. And, I promised myself I wouldn't do this. I promised myself I wouldn't let you see me break down because I want you to think I'm stronger than this. But, the truth is, I'm lost without you. Every day. Every single day is a struggle just to survive. I'm broken. Shattered. Destroyed without you. I want to be strong and get through this with grace and dignity, but you destroyed me. You broke me, Colt. And there's no point pretending I'll ever be okay with this." She stared at him as she choked the words out, allowing the tears she'd held in for so long to finally fall freely. Every thought she'd had since he walked away poured out of her.

He pulled her into his chest, rubbing her back and kissing her head. "Don't cry," he whispered in her ear. "I'm so sorry. Please don't cry."

"I just don't understand how you can just walk away. After everything we've gone through together. How can you just move on, move away and live with someone else like you never felt anything for me? Like we didn't have a life together. Dreams together. How can you just forget about me? I just really wish I knew how you did it, because *I can't.* I wish so badly that I could be like you, but I can't. I just miss you. All of the time. And it all just hurts. It hurts so badly: not being with you, not seeing you, not being able to tell you how much I love you every second. Because I do, Colt, I do love you. I love you and I miss you and...*are you even sorry*? Because you've never said it. You've never told me that you're sorry for the way you've done me. Not once. So, are you? I mean, *you have a kid.* A daughter. A...toddler? Is that what two-year-olds are? You told me you didn't want children. I always wanted them and you took that away from me. I'll never get a chance to be a mother now. And I was okay with that before, because you were all I needed. But, now I don't have anything. I'm all alone and you have this other family and you've just...discarded me." She was rambling now, every ounce of sadness and hurt pouring out of her like a tap that had been turned on.

He held her to his chest and she was sure she could feel his body shaking from his own sobs. He pulled her away from him suddenly and stared at her. "If you only knew how much I love you. Of course I love you. I love you every day. Every single day. Please, please, please...come back to me," he begged her, his eyes welling with tears.

She leaned into him, forgetting everything else and kissed him fiercely. He responded instantly, pulling her into him and lifting her up. He walked down the hallway, their lips locked together and her body in his arms. She kissed his face, his neck, smelling the smell she'd missed for so long. His faint cologne and the gel in his hair mixed together and brought her back to a simpler time. A time when the only thing that mattered was the two of them. A time without heartbreak and sadness. Her whole body pulsed in anticipation as he began twisting the bedroom door handle. He flung it open, barreling into the room and tossed her onto the bed. The room was dark, only a small amount of light from her window leaking in. She felt his hands moving up her waist as he slid down on top of her, kissing her from her beltline all the way up. When he reached her mouth, his kisses were gentle at first, easing into this old routine that somehow felt brand new. With each soft kiss, her passion grew, until she couldn't control herself anymore. She tore open her robe, pulling off his shirt and pressing their skin together. His skin burned her and his stubble rubbed her raw, yet she loved every minute of it.

When it was finally over, he lay beside her, rubbing his fingers across her skin. "I have missed you so much," he told her.

"Every day," she agreed.

"Every minute," he said.

"Every second," they said in unison. She laughed out loud, reaching for her robe from the floor. He stopped her, holding her hand.

"No, don't. Stay like this. Just...just stay."

So, she did.

# MONROE

When Monroe woke up the next morning, he was still there. She leaned in, wrapping her arms around his bare shoulders and kissed the back of his head, breathing in his warm, earthy smell. He stirred, rolling over to face her.

"Good morning." She smiled at him.

"Good morning." He kissed her arm, his eyes still groggy with sleep.

"Do you want me to make you some breakfast?"

"Breakfast would be nice." He glanced at the clock. "Oh, wow. I can't believe we slept in this late. I've got to be at the office soon. I'm going to go take my shower."

"Okay." She climbed out of bed, throwing on her robe. "Any preferences?"

"On the shower?" He smirked. "I like them hot."

"On breakfast," she retorted.

He winked at her, pulling her in for a quick kiss. "I like that hot, too." He grabbed hold of her robe strings, pulling at them playfully. "You can leave this off if you'd like."

She pulled back away from him, retying it. Her face

burned from his attention. It felt so good to have him touch her again.

He stood too, walking toward the bathroom. Before he reached the door, he turned to face her. "Hey, do you think you could find my toolbox? I'll go ahead and install that lock before I head to work this morning."

"Sure," Monroe said, though her happiness decreased at the thought of him leaving, even for a second.

His face softened, spying the look in her eyes. "Hey, don't worry. I'll be back. I promise."

She smiled halfheartedly, nodding, though she couldn't help wondering if he'd go to work or to see Jenna first. He walked back to her, kissing her forehead and pulling her into a quick hug before turning around and heading down the hall. She tucked a piece of her dark hair behind her ear before making her way into the kitchen. As she searched for a box of pancake mix, she put on a pan of bacon and eggs. From the cabinet, she pulled out chocolate chips and blueberries. It was Colt's favorite pancake combination.

As she cooked, she danced around the kitchen, listening to the shower running. It felt strange, grabbing two plates again. Having the need to cook for two people. *Strange,* she thought, *but perfect.* As the food cooked, she searched the closet where Colt kept his tools and pulled out his old toolbox. It felt like it had been years since she'd seen the old rusty thing—a hand-me-down from his father. She set it down on the counter, opening it and pulling out a hammer, nails, and a screwdriver. She wasn't sure exactly what he would need, but assumed she could cover the basics for him.

She heard the shower shut off as she was putting the food on their plates and felt butterflies fill her stomach. She turned around, plates in hand, and slammed straight into the island's counter, knocking his toolbox off the edge.

Tools plunged to the ground with a loud crash. She jumped back, the box barely missing her feet. She cursed, setting the plates down, and bent down to clean up the mess.

She heard his footsteps rushing toward her and shot up, banging her head on the countertop.

"Ouch!" she cried out in agony, covering her head. "Oh, god!" He entered the kitchen, towel wrapped around his waist, and reached for her instantly.

"What happened? Are you okay?" he asked, touching her head.

"I'm okay," she told him, trying not to wince.

He opened the freezer, eyes still on her, pulling out a bag of frozen peas and placing them on her head carefully. "Here you go. I've got these," he said, bending down to pick up the rest of the tools.

Feeling embarrassed, she set the bag of peas down and grabbed their plates, walking them over to the table. She pulled out a chair and took her seat, staring at her plate in shame, her face burning. Once the tools had been picked up, he joined her, handing her the bag of peas again.

"You should keep these on your head, sweetheart. It'll help with the swelling. Otherwise, it'll knot up."

Monroe nodded, taking the bag. Colt snatched a piece of bacon from the plate, chewing it quickly before standing up from the table. He dusted his hands off.

"This is delicious, babe. I'm going to go ahead and install your lock though, okay? I'll have to head to the office soon but I want to make sure it's in before I go."

"Okay." Monroe placed the bag on her head with caution. He kissed her gently before turning and walking out of the room. She took a bite of her eggs, the warmth filling her empty stomach. His phone lay on the island, beside the coffee pot. Without hesitation, she stood up, walking toward it. She wondered if Jenna had called him last night. She wondered if he'd told her why he wouldn't be home. Should she feel guilty for being the other woman this time? Could she even be the other woman if she was still married to the man? She pushed the thought from her mind, selecting the phone icon that indicated his call log.

Jenna had called him once the night before but there was nothing from this morning. Before that it had been days since they'd shared a call. She reminded herself, feeling the sting of the realization, that living together required fewer calls than if they were living apart. She exited the call screen, listening to make sure he was still working before she continued to search. She touched the messages icon. Her own name was nowhere in his phone at all. *He'd deleted her.* The pain of that discovery hung in the air as she clicked on Jenna's name.

The last text message was from two months before:

**Jenna: I miss you**

**Colt: I miss you more**

**Jenna: Could you pick up spaghetti sauce?**

**Colt: Yes, anything else?**

**Jenna: Wine please**

**Colt: Anything for you**

THEN, a week before that:

**Jenna: Tiffany is running a fever**

**Colt: Doctor?**

**Jenna: Not yet- waiting it out. Will you bring her home some juice though?**

**Colt: Of course, tell her that Daddy loves her. I'll be home soon.**

A FEW DAYS BEFORE THAT:

**Colt: Come here**

**Jenna: What?**

**Colt: Come here. I miss you.**

**Jenna: I'm just in the kitchen**

**Colt: I know...That's too far away from me. I miss you too much.**

A WEEK BEFORE THAT:

**Colt: Do you have a number for the restaurant to leave with the sitter?**

**Jenna: Google it**

**Colt: I did. Can't find it...**

**Jenna: Do people actually leave numbers for restaurants anymore? We have our cells**

**Colt: Oh yeah lol. My girl is so smart. Just nervous about leaving her**

**Jenna: It'll be fine. Love you**

**Colt: Love you. See you at Ellegio's**

**Jenna: Not soon enough**

**Colt: Never soon enough**

She put the phone down, her eyes filled with tears. These texts dated back months, when he'd still been living at home. Her home. Their home. All along, he'd been living this whole other life and she'd been completely ignorant to how far the deceit went. To some extent, she guessed she knew it—he did have a child after all—but seeing it there in black and white shattered what was left of her heart. Ellegio's, the restaurant he'd mentioned was the same place where he'd proposed to her. It was where they'd had their first date so many years ago. It had always been her favorite restaurant and she'd foolishly believed it was special and just for them. So much of their life together had happened there. Celebrations had been toasted over their white tablecloths and bad days had been made better with their cheesecake. It hurt her that he'd taken Jenna there, too. She stared at the phone, a ball of anger welling in her chest.

She heard footsteps coming up behind her and spun around, realizing she'd stopped listening to him work. He stood behind her, his clothes now on, tools in hand.

"Do you know where the—" he stopped short when he saw her face. "What's wrong?"

She looked up at him, her face burning, cool tears on her cheeks. "You took her to Ellegio's?" she asked, her voice shaking.

His jaw dropped open as his gaze darted toward the phone in her hand. "What? Did you go through my phone?"

"How could you?"

His face was emotionless. "Please just hand me my phone." His outstretched palm was waiting, but Monroe didn't move.

"Answer me, Colt! How dare you?"

"Last night was so amazing, please don't ruin that," he begged.

"Ruin that?" she asked, nearing hysterics. "How could I, Colt? How could I possibly ruin anything when you've already ruined it? You ruined everything the moment you betrayed me."

"I never betrayed you."

She scoffed, throwing his phone at him. It fell to the floor with a loud crash and she was sure it must've broken. "Get the hell out of my house."

He bent to pick up the phone, not even bothering to check to see if it was damaged. "Monroe, stop this. Please. I can't do this right now. Be sensible. I'll leave if you want me to, but let me install your lock first. Be mad at me all you want, but I'm going to make sure that you're safe." He reached for her, his voice calm.

She pulled away quickly, ducking out of his grasp. "Just get out," she told him sharply, snatching the lock from his hand. "I don't need you. I never want to see you again, Colt. All you do anymore is hurt me. Just *get out.*"

His face grew white as if she'd slapped him, his jaw tense, and he pressed his lips together. He pulled the hammer from his front belt loop and laid it on the counter. "Before you start handing out blame, take a good hard look in the mirror, Monroe. You were never the innocent one." With that, he was out of the kitchen and then out of the condo without another word.

"Look in the mirror?" she screamed after he was gone. "I've done nothing wrong here. Nothing!" She fell to the floor helplessly as she began to feel his absence, crying into her hands.

She sobbed for minutes on end, until each cry ached in her chest and her cheeks were sopping wet. There was nothing as painful as watching him walk away. Nothing as painful as knowing it could be, *should be,* for the last time.

Finally, she forced herself to stand up, making her way to the bathroom. She turned on the faucet, pulling the plug and allowing her bathtub to fill up. She slipped off her robe, sliding into the warm water with ease. It had been a long time since she'd allowed herself to soak in her garden tub. The water surrounded her and she lay still, her mind drifting away. Her head still throbbed from her accident, yet somehow it was her heart that she was concerned with. She tried hard to focus on anything else.

The house around her was still. She let out a sigh when, after a long time of soaking, she felt her hands growing wrinkly and stood up. She grabbed her razor. Her legs dripped water and she ran her hand down them, propping one foot up on the edge of the tub to get a good angle. She began shaving, feeling the patches of smooth skin underneath her fingertips, still lost in her own world.

She stared at her reflection in the water as something caught her eye. The foggy water didn't reveal much, but in its hazy reflection she could see the shape of her body. Just beyond it something was unfamiliar—a figure moving toward her.

She looked up, gasping, as he took a step further, causing her to throw the razor across the room. She let out a petrified scream, trying to cover herself with the shower curtain. He ripped it away from her, staring at her freely. One burly hand went around her mouth, muffling her screams. He jerked her from the bathtub, her ankles smacking loudly against the acrylic sides.

She cried out again, fear pounding in her chest as real as a heartbeat. She couldn't breathe, his hand covering her entire face. As she stared into his eyes, empty and menacing, she heard the purr of his zipper and the smack of his belt, warning her of what was to come. Her body was cold, both from the air on her still wet body and her paralyzing fear.

The linoleum squeaked under them with every move. She begged him to stop, tears and snot pouring down her face and onto his palm, but he didn't seem to notice. His eyes locked with hers, his rough skin rubbing against hers painfully as he began what he came here to do. Her body went rigid with the sudden familiarity of it all and suddenly she realized...she'd been here before.

# COLT

The first time Colt had ever witnessed his wife's dark days, it was long after they'd started occurring. Being a part of them for the first time, dealing with it firsthand, was enough to break his heart. It was the hardest thing he'd ever had to live through—something he wouldn't wish on anyone. Difficult as it was, it was an experience he could still remember in great detail. He'd come home from work that day to find her missing. He'd searched all through the house in a state of panic. When he'd finally found her, she was curled up in their closet, alone in the dark. She wouldn't look at him, wouldn't speak. She didn't come out for three days. To be honest, he couldn't even recall seeing her go to the bathroom. He brought food and water to her constantly, leaving it on the floor beside her. When he'd come back, hours later, nothing would be touched. He considered calling the police, bringing in someone to help him, but he was worried about what might happen to her. Nothing like what he was witnessing had ever happened to him before and he was terrified to do the wrong thing.

It was just a few months after they'd been married and she was so different than the person who he was used to, the warm, amazing woman he'd fallen in love with. He left the house on the second day, headed for work, feeling so angry that she wouldn't tell him what was wrong. He felt incredibly selfish, now, that he'd ever felt that way. That night when he'd gotten home from work though, he had realized it was much worse than he'd imagined. His wife was a shell of the woman he'd fallen in love with, the person he thought he knew. The next day, by some miracle, she was back. She acted as if nothing had ever happened and Colt struggled to find the right way to discuss it. Instead, it was never mentioned again.

The next time it happened, right after Tiffany had been born. She'd driven to the store to pick up a few groceries and didn't come home. That time, he didn't hear from her for over two weeks. Police were called, a search party was summoned, and Colt had feared the absolute worst. When she finally returned to him, it was as if no time had passed for her. She brought all of the soured groceries with her as if she'd only been gone a few hours, completely confused as to why they were all ruined.

He'd called Natalie then, terrified of what he should or shouldn't do—terrified of what she might do. "I just don't know what to do, Natalie."

"Whenever she does this, you just have to wait it out. I know it's hard. But she'll be home," she'd told him. "She always comes home."

She'd told him then what no one had told him before: that his wife was going to disappear for days and weeks at a time, mentally and sometimes physically as well. They had no idea what triggered her and there was no way to bring her back. It was all about waiting for her. She would return to him when she was ready. He simply had to be patient.

And so, he had. Colt had waited for her during her dark days and he'd held her when she'd come back to him. He'd loved his wife through something he could never expect her to love him through. Loved her through more than anyone should have to bear. And yet, he did. He did love her. More than he'd once thought humanly possible. She was his world —in the most literal sense. On days like today, it felt especially unfair that he'd fallen for someone so damaged. That his true love was someone who could never be wholly his. That she was a prisoner to her mind and, try as she might, some days she just couldn't win against it. He'd just wanted so badly to be normal: to go to work and come home and that be it. No extra drama.

He walked into his house, staring at the picture of him, Jenna, and Tiffany that hung on the wall. His family was beautiful, he knew, even with the dark shadows that loomed.

# MONROE

Monroe woke up to a loud thumping sound in her house. She sat up, realizing she was naked on the bathroom floor, though she wasn't sure why, and grabbed a towel. The bathtub was filled with water, she dipped her fingers in it and jerked back at the abrupt coolness. Dried blood trailed down her legs and she was strangely sore. She didn't remember her night with Colt being so bad, though she knew it had been quite a while for her. She touched her forehead, wondering if she'd tripped and fallen. She must have. Her face was incredibly sore.

The thumping noise came again and she realized it was a knock on the door. She dipped the corner of her towel in the water and used it to wipe the blood from her legs and the floor, sitting up the waste basket that had been knocked over. She grabbed her robe from the floor, ignoring its musty smell and strange stiffness and rushed toward the door, her legs feeling tired and unused.

Her hair had dried in a strange way, as if it hadn't been rinsed enough. In fact, it felt completely greasy. It would need to be shampooed again. Her right leg was only half shaved. What on earth had she done?

She opened the door, noticing the lock that Colt was supposed to install lying on the coffee table.

"Monroe?" Natalie exclaimed when she saw her. "Oh my god. What happened to you?"

"What do you mean?"

"You're all bloody, that's what! Your face is bruised! What the hell happened?" She stepped into the house, reaching for her patient and touching her lip. Monroe shouted out in pain she hadn't expected.

"Who did this to you?"

Monroe touched her own face, feeling the tender, bruised, and bloodied places. "I don't know."

"You don't know?" Natalie demanded. "You're all bruised up, Monroe. We have to get you to a hospital."

"No," Monroe said. "I don't need to go to the hospital. I'm fine. No one did this to me. I fell getting out of the bathtub. I'm just clumsy." She tried to laugh it off, yet now that she was conscious of her injuries, even a small smile hurt.

"You fell?" Natalie looked doubtful.

"Yes."

"Sit down, Monroe." Natalie gestured toward the couch. She did as she was told. "When did you fall?"

"A few hours ago," she said, trying not to make eye contact.

"Monroe, these bruises look really old. At least a day or two. There's no way you got them an hour ago." Monroe bit her lip. "Do you remember falling?" she asked lightly.

"No," Monroe answered her. "Not really."

"I didn't think so. This looks like a handprint." She traced a space along Monroe's lips with her fingers. "You really don't remember anything? You can trust me. You know whatever you tell me, I can't repeat it. I won't. Not to anyone. You can tell me the truth."

"I don't remember," Monroe reiterated.

A knock on the door caused them both to jump. She looked up, the light glaring in the window, to see Colt standing on the other side of the door. He pressed his face to the glass, trying to see into the dark living room.

"Colt?" Natalie called, rushing for the door. Monroe remained seated, her face firm. He shouldn't have come. Natalie opened the door, allowing him inside and Monroe kept quiet.

"Oh my god. What happened?" he asked, his eyes immediately locking on Monroe's face. She leaned back so he couldn't reach her as he stepped forward.

"When was the last time you saw her? Was she like this?" Natalie questioned him, a slight attitude in her voice.

"No, of course not," he said. "She was fine when I saw her. It was yesterday morning. I came by to install a lock. She wasn't...she didn't look like this. What happened?"

"A lock?" She raised her eyebrows.

"Oh, God." His face grew ashen. "Natalie, she called me. She said a guy came by. She was really freaked out. She wanted me to install a new lock for her. A deadbolt."

"A guy? What guy?"

"I don't know. She said she didn't know him. I couldn't get much out of her."

"So did you install the lock?"

"No," he said exasperatedly. "It's right there." He pointed to the lock, its partially opened package remained on the coffee table. "I tried to but we got into a fight. She asked me to leave so I did. I've been so worried about her all night, that's why I'm here. I came by first thing this morning to get it installed. I figured she would've cooled down by now."

"Seriously? You just left her?"

"She kicked me out!" he said defensively.

"It's your house!"

Natalie and Colt were at each other's throats when Monroe stood up. "It's *my* house and I'm right here!" she exploded at them.

"We know you're here, sweetheart," Colt told her, moving to her side. "I should have been here with you. This should never have happened. I shouldn't have ever left you alone. This is all my fault."

"Stop it!" Monroe pushed his hands away. "I'm not some damsel in distress, Colt. This isn't anyone's fault. I can take care of myself. I don't need you two here babysitting me."

"Monroe, who was here? Who did this to you? Do you remember?" Natalie asked.

"I told you." She shook her head. "I fell."

"You couldn't have fallen." Natalie stared at her, genuine concern in her eyes. "This doesn't look like an accident, the bruises are too precise. Where else are you hurt?"

Monroe shook her head again. "I'm completely fine," she insisted. "I'm getting older, I bruise easy. It happens, okay? So, just drop it, both of you." She turned, moving to the kitchen in an attempt to stop the interrogation. She grabbed the tea kettle off of the stove and filled it with water.

Natalie was behind her within moments, relentless as usual. "Monroe, who was here? When you bought the lock, I mean. Who was it that scared you?"

She tried to think back but it was as if a giant cloud had covered the memory entirely. She couldn't remember anything about that night. Unless Colt was lying about it. Maybe it hadn't happened at all. But why would he lie?

"Just a guy," she said, so tired of forgetting. "Probably a salesman. He just scared me. I'm sure I was overreacting."

"What did he look like?" Colt asked. "What did he say?"

"It's not important."

"It's not important or you don't remember?" Natalie asked.

She placed the kettle onto the stove top, turning around and resting her hands behind her on the counter. "What do you two want from me?"

"The truth, Monroe. We just want to know the truth," Natalie said firmly.

"I don't know what to tell you," she said, looking down at her feet.

"You don't remember what happened," Colt said. It wasn't a question.

Monroe, feeling horrified, shook her head. "I don't."

"Okay," Colt said, nodding his head firmly. He turned to Natalie. "What can we do? We have to figure this out. It's the only way to help her. Can we try hypnosis?"

Natalie shook her head, speaking to him under her breath. "Not unless she's receptive. You saw how it went last time. We can't push her, Colt."

"Last time?" Monroe asked. "What do you mean last time? Has this happened before? Wait," she said before pausing, suddenly feeling ill. "Natalie, how did you even know this was Colt?" Realization struck her as the two stared at each other with mortified looks. "Do you two know each other?" she asked. Neither answered at first, their eyes hurriedly glancing back and forth between each other and her.

"There are some things you should know," Colt said finally.

"Okay," Monroe said, not liking the ominous tone of his voice. "So, tell me."

"You should sit," Natalie warned her, pointing toward the kitchen table.

"I don't want to sit. Will someone just tell me what is going on? How do you two know each other?"

Natalie sighed. "Colt and I have known each other for a very long time, Monroe." She placed her hand on his shoulder, making Monroe's mouth grow dry. Colt patted Natalie's hand gently, smiling at her. They stared at each other for a moment too long, neither one seeming to know what to say.

Without warning, something in Monroe snapped as she realized what she was being told. She leapt forward, catapulting into Natalie and shoving her to the floor. Natalie screamed, trying to cover her face as Monroe's fists connected with her jaw. She rolled over under Monroe's weight, covering her head.

"*Monroe, stop it!* Stop this now! What are you doing? *What the hell are you doing?*" Colt yelled at her over the commotion, trying to pull her away from Natalie. Monroe was relentless, trying desperately to pry Natalie's hands from her face.

"How could you?" Monroe bellowed. "*How could you?*"

When he was finally able to lift her off, Natalie stood, touching her own bloodied lip with care. She patted her hair down, attempting to tame it. Staring at Monroe with wide eyes, she shook her head. "What the hell was that all about? What have I done?" she asked.

"Get out of my house, you whore!" Monroe yelled, spitting and foaming with every word. Her head pounded with anger, her whole body shaking.

"Whoa, Monroe." Colt grabbed her shoulders, turning her to face him. "Slow down a second. You're confused. What is it you think we're about to tell you?"

Monroe stared at him in disbelief. "That it's her. That she's who you've left me for, who you've cheated on me with. She's Jenna!" she shrieked the words, her whole body trembling with rage. Colt looked past Monroe to where Natalie-Jenna stood, a strange expression on his face.

"No." The word came from behind her. She spun around to face the homewrecker herself, ready to fight again. "No. I'm not Jenna." She paused, her eyes locked with Colt's for a second before coming back to Monroe. "I'm not Jenna, Monroe. You are."

# MONROE

Monroe sat on the couch staring at the blank wall. Everything that Natalie and Colt had told her floated around in her head, making no real sense at all. Her entire world was changing around her as she sat in dream-like state. Now that Colt had pointed out the places on the wall where the paint was a bit brighter, she could see the outline of the pictures that had once hung, yet she couldn't remember taking them down. He had showed her their wedding certificate, yet where her own name should have been, she'd written Jenna Jackson-Ray.

He had brought out the old wedding and family album, showing her pictures of the wedding she barely remembered. He showed her pictures of the day at the hospital when she'd given birth to their daughter, Tiffany Annalise Ray, only two years ago. He showed her the thin, silver scar on her lower stomach, further proof that what he was saying was true. But how could it be? How could any of it be true? How was it possible that she had memories spanning back over fifty years, yet according to the birth certificate he claimed was hers, she was only twenty-eight?

How was it possible that she could have feelings, thoughts, and emotions as Monroe, but never have actually been Monroe at all? She was Monroe. And yet, she was Jenna. But then, if she was Jenna, who was Monroe? Where did she come from? And if Jenna were to ever come back, where would she go?

# COLT

*The night his wife forgot herself was his worst nightmare coming true. Natalie had warned him that it could happen, that it had happened before, and yet he couldn't wrap his mind around the possibility. That night, he'd woken up to his wife screaming at him from the end of the bed. He sat up in a blurred, tired state, staring at her. "Jenna, what's wrong?" he asked, his voice coated with sleep.*

*"Who is Jenna?" she screamed at him hysterically, hurling a pillow his way.*

*"What?" he asked, his heart pounding. "What are you talking about? Calm down, you're going to wake Tiff up."*

*"What the hell are you talking about Colt?" she asked. "Are you cheating on me with some whore named Jenna?"*

*He stood up from the bed, walking toward her with his arms outstretched. It was as if she were playing a joke, yet her face showed no signs of laughter. "Hey, calm down, okay? Just calm down. We can figure this all out. Just please lower your voice."*

*"Screw you!" she bellowed. "We aren't figuring anything out. You need to get out of my house right now. Right now! How could*

*you do this to me, Colt? I've been faithful to you for nearly thirty years."*

Thirty years. *And just like that, he knew what was happening. His twenty-eight year old wife believed she'd been married to him for thirty years. Longer than she'd been alive.*

*He was losing her. He could see her slipping away and he wasn't sure where to grab to keep her with him. In her fit of rage, tears began to fall. He tried to approach her, his heart breaking at the sight of her tears and not knowing how to stop them.*

*"Sweetheart, please don't do this, okay? It's me. It's Colt. Come back to me. Come back." He turned around, grabbing a picture off of the night stand. "Remember this? Our wedding day. Three years ago. Not thirty. You remember this, right, Jenna?"*

*She smacked the picture from his hand without glancing at it, sending it flying across the room. "Get out," she repeated through gritted teeth. He stared at her, wishing it were all a bad dream. His beautiful, kind wife was staring at him as if he'd broken her heart and he couldn't explain that he hadn't. It took all of the strength he had to walk out of that room—to walk away from her. Everything. All he wanted to do was hold his wife, promise her that everything would be okay. Promise himself the same. Instead, he left, realizing he had no option at all.*

*He grabbed his jacket from the hall closet and Tiffany's jacket from the bench by her door, sneaking into her room and trying desperately not to wake her. He couldn't let her see her mother in this state. It would destroy them both. How was he ever going to explain to his daughter that one day her mother woke up and simply...forgot about her?*

# MONROE

Monroe walked into the bathroom, gathering up her dirty clothes from the floor. Her bloodied towel lay, dry and stained, on the floor. She bent down to pick it up carefully, extremely aware of her soreness. Something had happened in this room—that much she knew. Something to make her face bruised and swollen, and yet, try as she might, she couldn't remember it. She couldn't get past the thick cloud covering her memory. It was driving her crazy.

She walked to the laundry room, nearly tripping over the cat as he darted past, meowing at her for disturbing his sleep. "Oops. Sorry, Denny," she mumbled, tossing the clothes into the hamper.

The doorbell rang and she knew it would be Colt. He had told her he would stop by this morning with his daughter. *Their daughter.* How was it possible that she could see the girl and not remember her? That she could see the scar on her body yet not remember how it got there?

Ignoring her fears, she brushed a hand through her hair,

rushing toward the front door. The girl had her face pressed to the glass, waving ferociously.

"Mommy!" she yelled, recognizing her mother immediately. Her wavy black hair was pulled into a ponytail and she wore a purple dress with a cartoon character on the front. *Did Jenna know this cartoon character? Had she bought the dress? Where was Jenna?*

She opened the door and the girl latched to her leg quickly. "Mommy!" she cried again.

"Hello there," she told her, patting her head gently. Colt smiled at her, nodding to tell her it was okay. The girl pulled back, staring at her mother strangely, as if she knew she was an impostor. Suddenly, Denny launched himself into the room, letting out a loud yowl. The girl squealed.

"It's okay, he won't hurt you. That's—" Monroe began.

"Denny!" the girl screeched, hugging the cat. He purred, arching his back at her touch.

"Oh, right, of course," Monroe said softly, though the girl didn't seem to notice.

Colt, noticing the awkwardness, cleared his throat. "Tiff, why don't you take Denny to your room and let us fix your breakfast?"

"Okay." The little girl pouted a bit, but picked up the cat and headed to her room.

As soon as she was out of earshot, Colt gathered Monroe into his arms, his lips near her ear. "Hey," he whispered softly, petting her head. "You okay?"

She shook her head, looking up at her husband in confusion. "She knew Denny. She knew him, Colt, and he knew her...so why can't I remember her? She's my *daughter* and I can't remember a single thing about her. She might as well be a stranger. What kind of a mother does that make me?"

"Hey," he said, his voice harsh. "You are a great mother. You're just...you're sick right now. It's not your fault and I don't want you blaming yourself for any of it. None of this is your fault."

Tears fell down onto her cheeks as he rubbed her back. "It all feels like my fault. How is it possible to just forget your entire life? To forget who you are? Who you love? She grew inside of me, Colt. How could I just forget her?"

"I wish that I knew, sweetheart." He frowned at her sympathetically. "I really do. But we're going to figure this out. We'll get you back to us."

"No," she said, "you'll get Jenna back."

"Yes, but you are Jenna."

"No." She shook her head. "I mean, yes, I guess, technically I am. But I'm still Monroe. I have thoughts and feelings and memories as Monroe. What happens to me when Jenna comes back?"

He stared at her strangely. "I really don't know," he said after a moment. "I wish I did."

"Would it change anything?" she asked. "If I wanted to stay. Would it change how badly you want her back?"

"You. I want *you* back. *You are Jenna,*" he insisted. She leaned forward into his chest, smelling his woodsy cologne. She was so in love with his scent. Did Jenna feel the same way? She was having trouble deciphering which parts of herself were really her and which parts might come from Jenna.

"I don't understand," she told him.

"What don't you understand?"

She looked up at him then, into his eyes. "Why is it I can remember you? I don't remember anything about Jenna's life except that cat and yet...I remember you. You're still my husband. Even as Monroe."

He smiled at her warmly, kissing her forehead. "I'm your constant. Our love is stronger than anything, Jenna, it always has been. Ever since we met, it's been pure and amazing and so strong and I guess that deep down, no matter what, I'm there." He pointed to her heart. "No matter where your mind is...our love is right here. I'm right here."

She kissed him gently, through her tears, wishing anything could make sense. Anything besides how much she loved him. That part was absolutely clear. When they broke apart, he went on. "After you had Tiff, things got strange and your condition grew worse. You love our daughter very much, okay? But something changed in you that day. Natalie always thought you may forget her if we ever truly lost you. It has nothing to do with what kind of mother you are."

Monroe nodded. "I'm so sorry." She looked down, too embarrassed to meet his eye.

"You have—" He pulled her chin up, forcing her to look at him. "Look at me. You have nothing to apologize for. Nothing. What happened to you, whatever caused this, is not your fault. We know that. You need to know that too."

"Is she, I mean, is Tiffany...is she like me? Does she forget?" she asked, feeling a sense of worry overtake her at the possibility.

"No." He shook his head. "Natalie doesn't think it's genetic. Something like this...well, she thinks it's stress related. Trauma related. She thinks you may be trying to block out something that happened to you years ago."

"Something like what?" she asked. He touched the light bruises on her face, where she had overly applied makeup.

"I don't know, Jenna, only you can answer that."

# MONROE

Monroe woke up panting. She felt a bit of relief as she realized her husband's arm was still draped over her. She couldn't catch her breath in the too hot bedroom. Beside her, Colt was snoring peacefully. She remembered his snores as if he'd never left and silently vowed to never complain about them again. Carefully, she slid out from under his arm, pulling the covers over him so the cooler air wouldn't touch his skin; she didn't want to wake him.

She grabbed her robe from the rocking chair and slipped it over her shoulders, sneaking out of the bedroom as she tied it around herself. Her throat was completely dry and she needed water. She tiptoed down the hall, past the room where the little girl slept. She had helped Colt put her to bed earlier and kissed her goodnight like a mother should. She told her she loved her, but it all felt like an act. It was as if she were playing a character. As if she were playing Jenna.

She turned on the light in the kitchen and let out a yelp. He was there, waiting for her. He leapt toward her, his hand landing perfectly over her bruised lips.

"Shhh," he whispered teasingly to her, pressing his body into hers. "Be a good girl, Monroe."

Panic beat in her chest, loud and quick. She began hyperventilating as his hand slid down her side. His cologne burned her nose, making her head spin. Everything in her vision grew fuzzy as his fingers traced her neck, his lips tickling her ear. She felt as though she may throw up and her knees gave out under her with no warning.

"Please," she whimpered under his palm.

"Monroe, Monroe, Monroe...my sweet Monroe," he teased her, bending down with her as she sank. He scooped her up into his arms, carrying her to the couch and untying her robe with one hand. As his hands touched her bare skin with force, she remembered just how she'd gotten her latest bruises.

And then, just like that, she remembered everything.

# MONROE

It came back to her in flashes: some blurry, some clear. She remembered the first time it happened. She remembered *him*. He had been her sister's boyfriend and he'd come home with her from college one weekend to visit. Monroe remembered thinking he was cute with his dirty blond hair that stood up in every direction.

She remembered his smell, a cologne that made her want to buy a bottle and dump it on her pillow so that she could smell it each night. She'd been so jealous of her sister. So jealous of how happy they seemed. He'd been nice to her, he even stayed up playing cards with her long after everyone had grown tired and gone to bed.

Finally, when it became too late for her and she began yawning, he'd suggested they go to bed, too. She'd been reluctant at first, afraid to leave. She was terrified that he would wake up in the morning and forget that she wasn't just some dumb kid, forget about the fun they'd had together.

Eventually, though, she had to agree. He patted her

shoulder when she stood from the table, her skin tingling under his touch.

"Goodnight, kid," he said, flashing her a dashing smile.

"Goodnight," she said, her face heating up before she darted to her room, her head still dancing with memories of their night. She decided to sleep in the clothes she'd been wearing when she realized she could still smell his cologne on her. She went to sleep that night thinking about him. Dreaming about a future they could never have.

When she'd woken up later that night, she expected to see daylight coming in through her window. Instead, she saw only the glow of the streetlight through the blinds. Someone was laying on top of her. Still half asleep, she struggled to move but he stopped her, pressing his lips into hers. His metallic cologne filled her nose.

"Whoa, wait," she cried out, pulling back from him in shock.

"Don't move," he warned her.

"But, what are you doing?" She felt tears in her eyes. It was her first kiss, but it was all wrong.

"Just don't move, baby girl. You'll be fine. We're going to have a little fun." He kissed her again, his palms rubbing her arms.

"Please don't do this," she begged him, knowing then what was going to happen to her. He ignored her cries, pressing his hand into her mouth. She felt silent tears falling into his hand, frozen in place and praying desperately for someone to walk in—praying for someone to stop him.

"We need a nickname for you, baby. Something for me to call you when we have fun." He paused, thinking. She couldn't say a word. "How about Monroe? My sexy little Monroe."

She felt vomit rising up in her throat when suddenly the door swung open and he jumped off of her in an instant. It was too late. Her mother had seen what he was doing. She stood in the doorway, arms crossed, and stared at him, her face still.

"Come with me," she said after a moment, not glancing at Jenna. He did as he was told, following her mother out of the room. As the door closed, she curled up into bed, the weight of what had happened filling her. She felt sick, disgusting. No part of her body felt like her own anymore. It all hurt. She cried herself to sleep that night, though it took hours and when she woke up again, it was daylight.

She didn't remember what had happened right away, but as she grew more awake, it all came back to her. The sickening feeling was back in her stomach. She wanted to take a shower but she remembered someone talking about *it* at school. She remembered them saying that you shouldn't shower after. She couldn't remember why, but it seemed important. All she wanted to do was scrub every trace of him off of her skin. She didn't know if she could bear to face her sister, her mother must have kicked him out.

Would her sister be upset with her? Would she blame her? She walked out of her bedroom carefully, listening for voices. Would the police already be there? She shuddered at the thought. The silence in the house gave her goosebumps and her heart pounded in fear that he could jump out at any moment.

What if he hadn't left at all? What if he'd hurt her mother?

When she made it into the kitchen, her steps noisy on the old white linoleum, she saw her mother sitting at the table alone, a cup of coffee steaming in front of her. She stared into space, a blank look on her face, until Jenna came into view. She looked over at her daughter.

"Come sit down, Jenna. I made you some breakfast." She gestured to the plate of eggs and toast sitting across from her. Jenna followed her instructions, sitting down. Her mother was silent as she picked her fork up, scooting the food around and trying to find her appetite.

"Mom, I'm sorry about what happened—"

Her mother held her hand up, interrupting her. "We aren't going to talk about it, Jenna. We're *never* going to talk about it. And you can never tell anyone." Jenna gulped as her mother's shame-filled eyes bore into hers.

"Was it...what he did to me...was it—" She was unable to say the word. What an ugly word it was. Like a curse word she wasn't allowed to say. It hung in her throat, burning and scratching like a piece of dry toast.

"No." Her mother shook her head, understanding her question before she could finish it. "No, Jenna, it wasn't rape. You led him on. Staying up all night with a man twice your age. It's your fault just as well as his." The words stung and she tried not to blink as tears began forming in her eyes. "Your sister would never forgive you if she knew."

Jenna took in a sharp breath, knowing she'd be in more trouble if she cried. Her mother was right. This was all her fault. She looked down at her plate, sharp silence filling the room.

"Now, we aren't going to talk about it anymore I said." She stood up from the table. "Eat your breakfast."

---

Bits and pieces of the other times came back to her, too much to bear. Christmas breaks when he'd come back to the house, summer breaks, once when she was in college. She opened her eyes once more, his face above hers. His evil mouth smiled down at her, and in that moment she welcomed death, sure it would come soon. Praying it would. When it was over, he stood up, kissing her forehead once as he zipped his pants. He slid out the front door without a look back at her.

Once he was gone, she fell apart, tears soaking her pillow on the couch as sobs ripped her chest apart. Her whole body shook as she cried, a secret that had kept her whole for so long was now tearing her to shreds at its release. Her chest burned from lack of air as if the breaths she'd been taking her whole life weren't enough to sustain her anymore. She wasn't sure if she even cared.

She pulled her robe over herself, her hands quivering as she tied it. She kept picturing his face, yet she didn't know his name. It was still lost somewhere in her memories. His evil glare was burned into her memory. She heard footsteps coming down the hall and immediately feared the worst. Was he somehow back? She couldn't take it happening again; her heart would just give out.

Colt walked into the living room, rubbing his eyes from sleepiness. He stared at his wife, one eye closed. "Jen— er, Monroe? What are you doing up?" he mumbled.

Monroe let out a loud cry, partially from relief that it was only him, as she continued shaking inconsolably.

"What's wrong?" he asked, moving toward her, his arms around her immediately. He rubbed her hair under his palms, cupping her scalp.

"He was here," she said. It was the only sentence she could muster as she gasped for breath.

"Who was? Who was here, Monroe?" When she didn't answer, he went on. "Did he hurt you? What happened?" He begged her for answers, frantically trying to understand. She trembled in his arms, unable to speak. It was all too much. She prayed for him to understand without her having to say anything and she guessed somehow he did. "We need to call the police. You need to see a doctor," he told her gently, going into action.

He stood, picking her up. Her body was stiff in his arms but she let him hold her. He carried her down the hall to their bedroom, grabbing her clothes from the night stand. He laid her down on the bed, carefully slipping pants and then a shirt onto her and pulling off her robe. He held it in a ball under his arm.

"Can you walk?" he asked her. She stood carefully, taking a cautious step. Her legs felt weak under her but she could use them. She nodded.

"Colt." She held up her hand to stop him as he began to walk out of the room ahead of her. "No police."

"What are you talking about? Of course we're going to the police."

"It's my fault," she told him, remembering her mother's words.

He kissed her cheek gently, rubbing away a stray tear with his thumb, and shaking his head. "This could never be your fault." He held onto her hand softly, pulling her from the room.

Together, they walked into Tiffany's room. Colt picked her up from bed, slipping a blanket around her quietly. They walked out the front door, locking it behind them, and to the car. Once in the car, Colt buckled Tiffany into her car seat and began dialing a number into his phone.

A woman's sleepy voice answered through the car's speakers. "Hello?"

"Mom, it's Colt. We're going to bring Tiff over there for the night."

"What? What's wrong?" Her voice was instantly filled with concern.

"I'm taking Jenna to the emergency room. She was attacked." The word hit her. *Attacked.*

His mother's voice grew high in panic. "Attacked? What do you mean? Is she okay? Should I come there? I can meet you at the hospital."

"No, that's okay. I'll just drop her off. I don't want Tiff at the hospital in the middle of the night. We're about to pull down your street now." As he said it, they turned onto a quiet street and then into the drive of a small brick house. Monroe didn't recognize it. It was strange the way her memory was coming back to her in small pieces. The woman's voice had sounded familiar at least, yet this house seemed completely foreign. Her head hurt from her hurried, panicked thoughts. The voice inside her head was roaring. It seemed as though danger was lurking all around her.

Colt climbed out of the car, unloading their daughter into his mother's waiting arms. She waved at Monroe from the open doorway but Monroe couldn't muster the energy to wave back. She wasn't waving at her anyway. Not really. She was waving to Jenna. And Jenna was nowhere to be found.

Before she knew it, they were back in the car and the phone was ringing again. This time, he was calling Natalie.

"Hello?" Her groggy voice filled the car.

"Natalie, it's Colt. I need you to meet us at the hospital. Right now."

"Colt? What is it? What's wrong? Did something happen?" The tiredness in her voice disappeared immediately.

"Yes," he said, then paused as he took a deep breath. "Something happened. We need you."

"Colt, what is it? Is it Jenna? Is she okay?"

He nodded, though she couldn't see him. "Yes, it's Jenna. She's been attacked. We just...can you just please meet us there?"

"What do you mean *attacked*, Colt? Is she okay?" she asked hesitantly.

"Can you just meet us?" he asked, staring across the car at Jenna. She felt his gaze burning into her but couldn't meet his eyes.

"Yes, okay, fine. But, I don't know if the hospital is a great idea. Maybe you should bring her by my office first. I'm worried this will just overwhelm her. She needs to be around something familiar right now." Monroe looked to Colt, curious as to what he would decide.

"What? No. No way. I'll be right there with her but she's going to the hospital before she goes anywhere else. We have to get her checked out. Plus, I want the police to do one of those *kits*." He said the word softly to shield her, though she knew what he meant. "I want this guy caught."

"Okay." Natalie sighed. "You're right. Of course. I'll be there in fifteen minutes."

"Thank you," he said before a beep sounded, letting them know the call had ended and they were, once again, all alone.

# MONROE

Over four hours later, after Monroe had been poked, prodded, photographed, examined, dyed, measured, and had countless other excruciatingly painful things done to her; after the police had questioned her and taken their samples; after all of the shots and tests, only then was she allowed a moment of rest. So many hands had been on her, so many people looking at every part of her, that she now felt strange standing alone in the shower watching the steam rise. Colt had gone down to the cafeteria to get her a coffee. It was the first time he'd left her side all night.

She felt the bar of soap in her hand, scrubbing her skin so hard that it had turned a light shade of red. It still wasn't enough. She wanted every trace of the monster off of her. She cried and scrubbed, her tears mixing with the water until they disappeared. She sank down onto the ground, leaning against the cold plastic wall. The hot water splashed against her skin, burning her face, but she didn't move. She couldn't. This was the most peaceful she'd felt in a long time.

The door to the bathroom opened and a nurse walked in.

Monroe didn't bother covering herself, they'd all seen every inch of her over the past few hours.

"How are you?" the nurse asked. She looked up through the steady stream of water and steam, expecting to see an unfamiliar face. Instead, she saw Natalie.

"What are you doing here?" Monroe asked, standing up carefully. Her therapist stood in front of her, her knowing eyes full of sympathy. She held out a hand to Monroe, who graciously fell into her arms, soaking Natalie's clothes and the floor. Natalie didn't seem to notice or care. She held her, patting her back, for a very long time while Monroe remained lifeless.

When Monroe finally pulled away, turning off the shower, Natalie grabbed a towel from the shelf. "I'll help you dry off. Quickly. We're getting you out of here."

Monroe nodded, stepping out of the shower slowly. Natalie was gentle, patting every inch of Monroe's skin with the towel. She rubbed it between her shoulder blades, where she could still feel the fading bruises. Natalie helped her step into clothes she must have brought herself and gently eased her out of the room.

As they walked down the long hall, Monroe was sure her legs would give out at any moment, but they continued to work as Natalie led the way. When they got out of the hospital and to the car, Monroe climbed in without a word, though a million questions swam through her mind.

# MONROE

Natalie must've lived far from town, because they drove for what seemed like hours without stopping. When they finally arrived at her house, Monroe stared out the windshield with a blazing numbness. Nothing felt real to her anymore. She couldn't have slept if she'd wanted to and yet it felt as though she were in a dream.

"Where's Colt?" She managed to fumble out the question she desperately wanted to know the answer to. It was hard for her to form words, as her mind continued to fight to create simple thoughts.

"He's coming," Natalie promised her. Monroe nodded, allowing Natalie to help her unbuckle her seatbelt and lead her inside. Her home was small, smaller than she'd imagined it would be. She set Monroe down on a black leather couch before hastening out of the room. Monroe slumped back, wondering what could be taking Colt so long.

Natalie reappeared after a few minutes, stirring a glass of tea. "Here you go," she told her, sitting the cup down.

"Thanks." Monroe smiled at her politely, taking a sip. It

was a bitter tea that tasted nothing like she was used to, but still she drank. She seemed unable to quench her thirst.

"Now, tell me what happened," Natalie coaxed her. Monroe was silent, unable to speak about the night's events for even a minute longer. "Monroe, please. You need to talk to someone who understands. You have to let it out." Again, she was silent. "Do you remember who he was? What he looked like?"

Monroe nodded. "Yes." Unlike every time before, his face was burned into her brain. She was unsure how she could've ever forgotten it in the first place.

"Can you describe him for me?" Natalie urged her, her eyebrows raised. Monroe shook her head, taking another sip.

"I can't. I'm sorry, Natalie. It hurts too much. I just...it's all still fresh right now."

Natalie nodded. "Of course it is. Of course." She patted Monroe's shoulder gently. "Go on and drink up. I'll run and get you a blanket so that you can rest. You must be exhausted."

Before Monroe could protest, Natalie was out of the room. She stared around the small living space, the walls lined with pictures of landscapes and faraway places. She couldn't help but notice that none of the pictures were of Natalie herself or any of her family. In fact, nothing in the room seemed personal. Pulling her from her thoughts, keys jingled in the front door, causing Monroe to jump and spill her tea. She used the sleeve of her shirt to try and clean it up, hurrying before the door swung open. She hoped it would be Colt. As the door finally opened, Natalie walked back into the room, her eyes wide.

Both women looked to the doorway, where a woman with two paper sacks balanced on one arm stood. Her fuzzy gray hair stood up in every direction and her wrinkled, translucent skin dangled loosely off the bones they should've been attached to. She eyed Monroe, who stared right back with a menacing glare. Her throat grew dry the longer she stared.

"You're early," Natalie said, her voice stern yet nervous.

The woman's face was rigid. "Obviously. I couldn't keep waiting. Is he here yet?"

"He who?" Monroe asked. Did this woman know Colt?

"No," Natalie answered firmly. "He'll be here soon. You shouldn't have come until I was ready."

"Did you give her—" the woman asked but trailed off before finishing her thought, her eyes darting sideways at Monroe.

Natalie nodded, looking uncomfortable. Monroe stood up, a wave of nausea hitting her instantaneously. "Monroe," Natalie cautioned her. "You shouldn't stand. You're still very weak."

At her word, Monroe sat, feeling her world begin to spin. She opened her mouth, trying to speak, but her face felt numb. She reached to cover her mouth, her eyelids suddenly feeling all too heavy, but found she couldn't lift her hands. They seemed to weigh fifty pounds each. As her hands grew heavier, she realized her head was also too burdensome to keep up. She let it drop onto the couch behind her. She felt her eyes beginning to close, the last thing she could see clearly was Natalie and the woman staring at her in unison, strange looks on both of their faces.

"Monroe?" She heard Natalie speak her name, but her brain grew too blurry to form words as she felt her head sink further into the couch and then she was out.

# MONROE

When Monroe awoke, her mouth was dry and her head throbbed. She blinked her eyes, trying to see around in the dark room. She lifted her head, rubbing the dried drool off of her cheek, and trying to remember where she was. How much time had passed?

Sitting up, she realized she was in a bed, a comforter and sheets wrapped tightly around her.

She kicked her legs, attempting to move but found she couldn't get them loose. Panicking, she lunged forward, throwing the covers back and glancing at her legs. In the pitch black room, she couldn't see anything, where the room started or ended or who else might be in there with her.

"Hello?" she called out, her voice shaking. Her legs were tied down, though she couldn't tell to or with what. She heard footsteps that had her frozen in her spot, unsure where they might be coming from.

The door to the room that she was in opened, a bright light blinding her, and a dark figure passed through. She couldn't be sure of whether they were coming toward her or leaving. Her breathing grew quicker as she tried to remain still, her dry throat ached as she tried to keep her breaths contained. Heavy footsteps approached the door once more and it was swung open with a loud bang.

Natalie stood in the doorway, a tray of food in her hands. "Monroe, I'm so glad to see that you're awake."

"Where am I?" Monroe asked, her voice feeling foreign and unused in her throat.

"You're in my guest bedroom. I had my husband bring you in here once you fell asleep. Here." She offered her a drink from the tray before setting it on the bedside table. "I brought you a drink. Some food too."

Monroe frowned, eyeing the drink cautiously, though unable to deny her thirst. "Where's Colt?" she asked. "Why hasn't he come to get me? How long have I been here? Why am I tied up?"

Natalie held her hands up. "Shh, slow down now. Colt is at work. He's been to visit you a few times but you've been asleep for several days. We tied you up so that you wouldn't try to get up and hurt yourself. You're very, very weak right now, Monroe, and we couldn't watch you constantly to make sure you stayed in bed. It's important that you get your rest."

"Can I talk to him?" she asked, not sure she believed the story. Something didn't seem right about what Natalie was telling her. "I feel fine."

Natalie placed her hand on Monroe's shoulder. "You're a fighter. I admire that about you. But, you don't have to fight right now. The doctor said you need around-the-clock care. Colt just can't give that to you on his own. He's got his job and Tiffany to take care of. I'm sure he'll be back here in a few hours though. Don't worry. He's never gone long. He's very protective of you, you know."

"Can you at least untie me? Please. This is ridiculous."

Natalie looked uneasy. "I'm sorry, Monroe. I don't think that is a good idea right now. Here—drink up. Eat some toast. You'll feel better." Monroe took a sip of her water to appease her host. The drink tasted sour, almost coppery, but she didn't let it show. "There, that's good. You need to get your energy back up." Natalie smiled at her. "Then we can get you out of bed and back home."

"Who was that woman?" Monroe asked, her memory coming back. "Have they caught the man who attacked me?"

"No," Natalie answered. "The police don't have much to go on. They didn't find any DNA on you and your memory from that night is foggy at best, which is completely understandable. The truth is, right now, there's little chance he'll ever be caught."

Monroe bit her lip, trying hard not to show the hurt on her face. "What about the woman?"

"Was there a woman?" Natalie raised her eyebrows.

"The night that I was attacked, you were talking to a woman. She was older. Gray hair, haunting eyes. It's the last thing I remember."

Natalie shook her head; her face showed only confusion. "There was no woman, Monroe. It was only me and you that night."

"No!" Monroe insisted, her skin growing cold. "She was here. I saw her! I swear she was here."

"Sweetie, you had a lot of pain medication that night. It's possible you don't quite remember everything correctly. It wouldn't be the strangest thing if you'd hallucinated or even had a very vivid dream."

Monroe shook her head. "That can't have been it. It was all too real. I know what I remember."

"Hallucinations often seem very real. As real as me talking to you right now," Natalie told her. Monroe shook her head again, her mind racing. She could still see the woman's face: her all-knowing eyes surrounded by deep wrinkles, her wild, gray hair that seemed to fly in every direction.

"Monroe," Natalie said finally, her voice filled with concern. "We can talk about what you think you saw if you want to. Do you remember what she looked like?"

In that moment though, despite the picture being clear as day in her mind, Monroe couldn't answer.

"Monroe," Natalie said again, fear in her eyes. "Did you know the woman?"

*No.* She shook her head to answer but the voice coming out didn't cooperate. Instead, the word she heard herself saying was "Yes."

# JENNA

Jenna woke up in a dark room. She reached over to touch her husband but was surprised to find only empty space. How in the world had she ended up in a twin-sized bed? Where was Tiffany?

"Colt?" she cried out, sitting up on the bed. She tried to climb out but panicked when she realized her legs were tied down. "Colt!" she screamed out. *Where is he?* she wondered. *Better yet, where am I?*

The door to the room she was sleeping in opened and a light switched on. Her sister stood in front of her. "Natalie?" she asked, a sigh of relief pouring out of her. "Oh, thank god. Natalie, what's going on?"

"Jenna?" Natalie asked, her eyes wide in shock, as if she hadn't expected to see her there. "Is it really you?"

"Of course it's me. Who else would it be? What is going on? Where are we?" Jenna asked, her hands pulling at the ties that held her down.

Natalie kept her distance, as if she were afraid of her own sister. "Jenna, you have to be quiet."

"What are you talking about?" she asked, not bothering to lower her voice. "Where is Colt? What is happening? Why am I tied up?"

Suddenly, Jenna heard footsteps coming toward the bedroom, heavier than Natalie's had been but from further away. Natalie heard them too and seemed to panic. She grabbed hold of the ties that held her sister's legs, ripping them off feverishly. "You have to get out of here," she told her quickly.

"What are you talking about? And where the hell is *here?*"

"I don't have time to explain. Jenna, you aren't safe here. You have to go. Now." She stood her sister up with force, pushing her into a small bathroom off the bedroom. "Climb out the window, Jenna. Don't look back, okay? Climb out the window and run until you find someone to help you." She wrapped her sister in a quick hug. "It's so good to see you."

"I don't understand—" Jenna begged her for an answer, hugging her back.

Natalie pushed her further toward the window, interrupting her. "I know and I'm sorry. There's no time. Don't tell anyone where you were, Jenna. Do you hear me?" Jenna nodded, though she didn't understand at all. "And don't come back. No matter what. Now go!" She hoisted her little sister up onto the toilet and out the window in a rush, shutting the window behind her.

Jenna looked around the dark yard, wondering where on earth she could be. She had no cellphone and no way to contact Colt. Listening to her sister's warnings that played in her head, she began running, though her legs did not seem to want to carry her. Her whole body felt sore, as if it hadn't been used in months. It was like she was living in some crazy dream. She didn't recognize any of her surroundings.

She felt her bare feet crunching on dry leaves in the yard and jumped up in pain as her foot connected with a pine cone. She looked back to face the house as she saw the porch light flip on behind her and heard voices. Turning back around, she picked up the pace, running into the tree line just as three flashlight beams shone into the darkness. She tripped, plunging herself straight into the bark of a tree. As she stood up, she held her breath, trying hard not to let out a painful cry. Anxiety grew in her, though she wasn't sure why she was nervous or why Natalie had told her to run in the first place. She heard their cries growing closer, yelling out her name. Natalie was yelling with them, one man and another woman. She was sure she recognized the voices. She considered responding to their calls at first, but Natalie had made her promise not to turn back and so she wouldn't.

She ran, zigzagging through trees and stumbling over limbs and overgrowth. Finally, when she felt like she could run no longer on her sore and wobbly legs, she saw headlights zooming past. She'd come to a highway.

She darted into the road without a second thought, ignoring her impending death and the fact that she was dressed only in an oversized nightgown. She held up her hands, begging the truck in front of her to stop. The driver hit his brakes, squealing the tires as he slid closer to her than she would have liked.

When he came to a complete stop, Jenna approached his passenger's side door. The driver was an elderly man, a red, worn baseball cap on his head and a plump belly bursting out of the pearl snaps on his flannel shirt. His long gray hair fell down below his shoulders.

He spoke in a gruff voice, staring at her with a nervous expression. "Is everything all right, ma'am?"

"No," she told him honestly. "Can you please tell me where I am? I need to get home to my husband. I...I woke up in the woods." She pointed behind her, thinking quickly.

He leaned over, pushing his passenger's side door open. "You'd better climb in. It's freezing out tonight. I'll let you use my cellphone to call your husband."

She nodded gratefully, praying in the back of her mind that he wasn't a serial killer. She didn't have time to worry about it, though, as she climbed into the heat of his car.

"Now, where do you live? Do you want me to take you to the hospital? You're covered in blood." He frowned at her, looking down at her legs which were covered in scrapes and scratches from her narrow escape.

She graciously took his cellphone when he offered it, dialing Colt's number from memory. "No, I'm all right. I'm just a bit scraped up from running through the woods. It's nothing a Band-Aid won't fix. I'm so sorry about this. I'm getting blood everywhere." She reached down, trying to wipe the blood off her legs with the corner of her nightgown.

"Don't be sorry, it'll wash out, just as long as you're okay. Let's just get you home." He reached over her, digging in his glove compartment, pulling out a handful of napkins and handing them to her to clean herself up. She wiped her legs down, wincing in pain as each touch burned more than the last against the rough paper.

Colt's line rang and rang. On the third ring, he answered. His voice sounded distant. "Hello?"

"Colt?" Tears hit her eyes as she heard his voice, feeling as if it had been so long since she'd heard it.

"Who is this?" he asked cautiously.

"Colt? It's me, it's...it's Jenna."

"Jenna?" She heard his voice break then, soft tears and

muffled breaths filling the line. "Jenna, oh thank god. Where are you?"

Jenna looked at the street sign up ahead. "I'm on I-55. I'm so confused, Colt. I woke up in the middle of nowhere. I don't know how I got here."

"Can I come get you? I need you to stay right where you are. Are you safe?"

She looked at the driver who was staring straight ahead in what looked like an attempt to give her privacy. "Yes, I'm safe. I'll stay here."

"What mile marker are you near? Headed in what direction?" Colt asked. Jenna relayed the question to the man.

"We're just past mile marker 261, headed south," she repeated his answer to Colt.

"Who are you with Jenna?" Colt asked, sounding leery.

"I don't know..." she answered honestly. "I'm sorry. What's your name?"

"I'm David," the man told her.

"I'm with David," she said.

"Okay, don't leave that spot. Don't go anywhere, Jenna. I'm on my way right now. I'm coming to get you, okay?" She heard his keys jingling through the line as if to prove his point.

"Okay, please hurry," she begged. She closed the old flip phone, handing it back to David. "Thank you," she said, opening the car door.

"Where are you going?" he asked.

"My husband is going to pick me up here. I can't thank you enough for helping me. I don't have any money with me but if you want to give me your address I can happily send you something for your time. Just write it on a napkin so I don't forget."

The man held up his hand to stop her and Jenna flinched. "Look miss, I don't want your money. What I do want is for you to stay in the car until your husband gets here. It's too cold and dangerous for you to be out here alone."

Jenna bit her lip. "Oh, I couldn't possibly bother you to stay. I'm sure that I'll be fine."

"It's no bother, honestly," he assured her. "I wouldn't feel right leaving you here unless I knew that you were safe."

"Are you absolutely sure? I hate to ask you to do that. You've already done more than enough."

"You aren't asking. It ain't an offer either. I'm telling you that I'm staying until you're safe and warm. A busy interstate is no place for a young thing like you to be wandering around in the middle of the night."

"Thank you," she said, feeling overwhelmed by his kindness. Without another word, she closed the door and pulled her legs up onto the seat. She continued trying to stop the bleeding from her legs; some of the cuts appeared to be deeper than she'd initially realized. David cranked up the heat, leaving her alone with her thoughts.

# JENNA

When Colt finally arrived at the place where Jenna was anxiously waiting for him, he ran to her, scooping her up with delicate hands as if he were afraid she may break.

"Oh, Jenna," he whispered, his face in her neck. His beard was longer than it had been, grayer even. She knew it could have only been a day or so since she'd seen him, yet he felt unfamiliar to her.

She hugged him tight, finally feeling safe. "Where's Tiff?" she asked. He brushed a piece of hair from her eyes.

"She's with my mom," he told her. "I didn't want her to have to be a part of all of this."

Jenna nodded, staring at the police officers who were standing just behind Colt. They were questioning the man who had probably saved her life about how he'd found her. When the officers finished talking with David, they approached her.

"Ma'am, we're going to need you to go with us to the

hospital. We can take your statement there," one of the officers said.

"Hospital? Statement? Is that really necessary? I'm fine," she insisted.

The woman officer sighed, looking to her partner and then back to her. "Your feet are bloody and bruised up. You have ligature marks on your ankles and you were found in the woods with no memory of how you got there or where you've been over the last week."

"Week?" Jenna asked in genuine shock.

"I'll drive her to the hospital," Colt told them, touching her arm cautiously. "We'll follow you."

The officer and her partner nodded, returning to their car. Colt turned, shaking David's hand again. "I can never thank you enough," he told him.

David nodded. "Of course. No thanks necessary. I'm just glad it all turned out okay." He looked at Jenna then, his face stern. "You take care of yourself, you hear?"

---

On the way to the hospital Jenna told Colt what she remembered: about the woods, about her escape, and about her sister. Colt listened patiently, allowing her to relive the story as it came back to her. He held her hand, rubbing his thumb against the back of it.

"Jenna, I've missed you so much. I'm so glad you're back," he said, his voice quiet.

"I missed you too, sweetheart," she said. "I can't believe I've been gone for a whole week. I don't remember anything except today. How is that even possible? Maybe Natalie can fill in the blanks for me, do you think?"

"I don't know. Maybe. Hopefully."

"What's wrong?" Jenna asked, sensing a strangeness in the air between them.

"Jenna, a lot has happened since I saw you last." He wasn't looking at her as he spoke, not even once. It worried her more than she liked to admit.

"Okay..." she said warily. He was quiet, not bothering to explain. "Are you going to tell me what that means?"

He frowned, pulling his hand away from hers to grip the wheel. "Well, you should just know—what you think you remember may not actually be what happened."

"What does that mean?" she asked, her voice cracking.

"For instance, you said you've been with Natalie this week." He raised his eyebrows at her.

"I didn't say this week, I said I was with Natalie *this morning*. I told you I can't remember being gone for a week."

"Well, either way, that's impossible, sweetie. Natalie lives over 40 miles in the opposite direction of the way you said you'd come from. Plus, I've seen Natalie every day this week. We've been going crazy looking for you after you disappeared from the hospital. It almost destroyed her that she never made it to see you. If she'd been with you this morning, there's no way she wouldn't have called me."

"Disappeared from the hospital? Colt, what are you talking about?"

"It's a long story, Jenna," he whispered as he turned the car into the hospital parking lot. "But, it all starts with the fact that it has been much longer than a week since anyone saw you."

# JENNA

Jenna sat in the hospital room, staring at the paisley pattern on the chair in between her legs. Across from her, Colt and Natalie sat, explaining everything again. Jenna's throat felt strangely tight.

"None of this makes any sense," Jenna said softly. She looked up, hoping to see a joking smile on their faces. Instead, Colt's face contained a worried grimace, while Natalie stared at her with a solemn expression.

"I know," Colt said finally.

"I mean, I don't remember any of it. Two months of time have passed and I can't recall a single day from that time. Yesterday for me was the day we ate spaghetti for dinner and Tiffany spilled her whole plate on the floor. We went for a walk after work. I can still remember it in such detail. How is that possible?"

"We don't know, Jenna," Natalie answered. "Your mind is very fragile right now. I think it's time to have you admitted to the hospital for further testing. I don't know what else to do."

"What?" Jenna asked. "No! You can't do that. They'll lock me up like some alien and run tests on me. You can't!"

Colt jumped up, sensing her panic, and wrapped his arms around her. "It's okay, Jenna. It hasn't been decided yet. We don't have to." He whispered the words in her ear, rocking her back and forth like a child.

Natalie spoke up then. "Colt, could I see you outside for a moment?"

Colt let go of her arms, turning to face Natalie. "Can't it wait? She's upset right now."

"No. I don't think it *can* wait," Natalie said firmly.

He sighed, shaking his head. "I'll be right back." Kissing Jenna's forehead quickly, he turned to leave the room. Jenna stared at them as they left, feeling incredibly alone. It was as if her husband and Natalie had formed their own little club. A club she wasn't invited to join. She could hear their hushed voices just outside of the door, though try as she might she couldn't make out what was being said. She burned her gaze into the door, focusing on their quiet tones. Nothing about this seemed real. She desperately needed answers, yet these were not the ones she'd been expecting. And they certainly weren't welcome. She walked over to the paper-lined examining table, climbing up onto it and lying back, hearing the paper crinkle under her weight.

---

When Jenna awoke, the room was dark. She saw a small light blinking beside her bed and heard a quiet beeping sound. Where was she? She tried to sit up but felt a sharp twinge of pain in her arm. Warm liquid was oozing over her skin slowly. She cried out, grasping her wrist in pain. Her skin burned with an unfamiliar sting, tears forming in her eyes suddenly.

"Help!" she cried out. "Help!" She looked around the dark room desperately, dread filling her. "Colt! Colt! Please help!" At first, it seemed no one would answer her cries, but finally the door swung open and a young nurse entered the room. The light came on instantly. The nurse took one look at Jenna, her eyes wide, before rushing to her side. Jenna looked down, staring at the blood pooling out of the cut on her wrist, the bloody IV needle laying beside her. Before she had time to react, the nurse had thrown on gloves, grabbing wads of gauze and pressing them to the wound. It was incredibly deep and the blood wasn't slowing.

"Keep still," she instructed. Jenna did as she said, tears beginning to fall down her cheeks. She tried to remain as still as possible though her wound really stung. After a few moments, the door flew open again and more nurses entered followed by a middle aged man wearing a white coat, the doctor.

"I found her like this," the first nurse told them.

"Jenna?" her doctor asked, staring at her with wide eyes. One of the nurses began rubbing alcohol over her wound, cleaning the area to check for where the cut began and ended. The others bustled around, pulling her sheets back and adjusting machines. When the door opened the final time, it was Natalie and Colt who walked in, their smiling faces immediately turning ghost-white.

"What happened?" Colt asked.

A nurse held her hands up, moving from Jenna's bedside to the door and shaking her head. "No. You can't be in here. I'm going to have to have you wait outside."

"But what happened? What is going on?" Natalie asked, not moving.

"Is she going to be okay?" Colt asked. Jenna stared at him from across the room, wanting desperately to be able to talk to him, for him to hold her and make her feel like it would all be okay.

"Please just wait outside," the nurse repeated, frustration in her voice. She shut the door, forcing them out as the doctor approached Jenna with a small bowl and a suture kit.

"Now then," he said, "let's get you fixed up." He took a syringe from one of the nurses, placing the needle on Jenna's arm, just above her wound. "You are going to feel a small pinch. This is just to help numb you."

Jenna watched as he wiped away her blood, the nurse who had been trying to stop her bleeding let go and allowed him to stick her several times around the laceration. He laid down the syringe, picking up a needle from the bowl, and sticking it through her skin before she was completely numb. He began sewing her up carefully. She watched the thread run through her thin, nearly transparent skin as if it were a quilt. The doctor's hands moved seamlessly, with the quiet endurance of someone who'd done this too many times. He patiently wiped away her blood as it continued to pool out. Finally, once her wound was sealed, he stopped, examining his work.

"There. Now, that's much better." He smiled at her, patting her shoulder. The mess around her was cleaned up quickly and then someone was helping her into a wheelchair that she hadn't noticed being brought in.

One nurse stripped her bed as another unhooked her remaining IV. The doctor opened the door then, stepping out and addressing a terrified looking Colt in a hushed voice. Jenna could see Natalie too, through the doorway, pacing beside them.

Her arm had finally grown numb, minutes after she'd needed it to. She stared down at the black stitches against her pale skin, feeling oddly at peace. The nurse pushed her chair out the door and toward Colt. He had tears in his eyes, leaning down to meet her immediately.

"Oh, Jenna," he said softly, rubbing her hair. "What have you done, sweetheart?"

The doctor spoke up. "This will only be temporary, we hope, Mr. Ray. Our doctor will want to speak with both of you after he examines her, of course. That won't be until morning, I'm afraid. You can both go home and get some rest in the meantime. She'll be safe here."

Jenna looked up at him in confusion. Colt stood, facing the doctor and shaking his head. "No. I want to stay with her. She shouldn't be alone."

The doctor pressed his lips together, showing small signs of frustration. "That won't be allowed. She'll be under twenty-four hour supervision in psych but until she's been seen by our psychiatrist on call, she won't be able to have visitors. It's protocol."

"I'm sorry, but what are you talking about? I'm not a visitor, I'm her husband. She needs me right now." Colt's face grew red as he tried to hold back tears.

Natalie grasped his arm gently, rubbing it. "Colt, it's okay. It's what she needs right now." She nodded toward the doctor. "It's okay, I've got him."

With that, the doctor nodded, appearing to be unaffected by the situation, and gestured for the nurse to go on. She began pushing the wheelchair carrying Jenna down the hall.

As if it were a warning, a prelude to the danger that lay ahead, her arm began to ache as the numbing sensation faded away. Tears brimming her eyes, she turned around in her chair slightly, trying to catch a glimpse of the two people she hoped would save her. They didn't move.

# JENNA

Jenna stared at the window in her room, up high enough that she could only see sky. The small, white room she'd been imprisoned in was far from calming. It made her skin crawl. She sat on the tiny, uncomfortable bed. Her mind seemed like a foreign place to her as she explored it, searching for answers as to where she had been. It had been two days since she'd been placed in the room, her only contact had been with a doctor and the few nurses who brought her food. She was alone.

Her doctor was a straight-to-the-point sort of man. He had explained to Jenna that what was happening to her was a fairly common thing. He'd said it was nothing to be ashamed of and he'd promised her he'd do everything he could to help her. He said that she was only there for her own protection. Everything he'd said to her felt scripted, as if he'd said it a dozen times already that day. She knew she was just another patient to him—another nuisance that he had to deal with.

Eventually, he'd left, explaining that he'd be back soon to check on her. He hadn't come back though, not yet. She waited for Colt to come visit her, to bring Tiffany to see her, but he hadn't.

She wanted to see her daughter so badly that it hurt, longed to run her fingers through her dark hair, to tickle her little belly. How was it possible that she could miss another person so much?

On the third day, the doctor came back. Natalie and Colt were with him this time. They crowded into her tiny, too-white cell, staring at her curiously.

"Could I?" Colt held his arms out to her, yet his eyes were on the doctor. Before anyone could answer, Jenna lunged forward, throwing herself into his arms. She breathed in the familiar earthy scent of him, her heart finding a peace it hadn't known in so long. Her tears soaked through his gray t-shirt, his arms rubbing her gently.

Around them, the room was silent, allowing them to just be together. He lowered his face to hers, kissing her forehead and then her cheeks before finding her lips. He pulled away before she realized what was happening, the moment suddenly gone. He touched her shoulders gently, staring into her eyes, his cheeks bright red.

"I've missed you so much," he told her.

"I've missed you too. Take me home," she begged him. Without answering, Colt stepped back. Natalie approached her next, her arms outstretched.

"Hey, baby sister." She hugged her, rubbing her hair. "It's so good to see you again."

"It's good to see you too. You guys have to get me out of here. You have no idea what this place is like." Natalie stepped back, smiling at her sadly but not agreeing.

"Well then, Jenna," the doctor said, "why don't you tell us

all what it has been like in here for you. Tell us how you've been feeling."

"Bored." Jenna stared at him. "Scared. Alone." The doctor nodded but didn't speak, so she went on. "I don't understand why I'm here or what is going on. Nothing about this makes sense to me. And I'm so hurt that you guys just left me here." She choked back tears as she tried to finish her sentence, staring at her family with pain in her eyes. "I needed you. I needed you both and you just...left me."

"We didn't have a choice, Jenna. You know I'd never leave you if I didn't have to. I've thought about you every single day. Every second. It's killing me to leave you here," Colt told her.

"Don't you see, Jenna? We never meant to hurt you. We only wanted to keep you safe," Natalie said softly.

"Keep me safe? How is this keeping me safe?" She gestured to the walls around her, more a prison than a sanctuary. The room fell silent, each of her guests looking uncomfortable. "Well?" she demanded when no one seemed to have an answer.

"Jenna, after you disappeared, you were gone for days. Dehydrated. Starving. You have no memory of where you were or what happened to you," Colt said finally.

"I told you I was with Natalie," Jenna roared at him.

"No." Natalie shook her head. "No, you weren't. I hadn't seen you, Jenna. No one had. We'd been looking for you all that time. You just disappeared again."

"Disappeared? No!" Jenna cried. "I remember being with you. You told me to run away."

"You aren't remembering clearly, sweetheart. You thought it had only been a day. You'd been gone for so much longer…" Colt said sadly.

"But—"

"And after everything that has happened here, we can't risk you being alone right now."

"What?" Jenna asked, shocked. "What the hell does that mean? Are you afraid I'll disappear again?"

"We can't risk you hurting yourself again," Natalie said calmly, staring at her.

"What? Hurting myself? Again? I would never do that. You think I did this on purpose?" Jenna screamed, holding her wrist up. It was as if the air had been ripped from her lungs. The thought hadn't even occurred to her that they believed her wound was self-inflicted.

"But you did, Jenna," her doctor said.

"No!" she insisted. "The needle must have slipped out of my arm. It had to. I promise you, I didn't do this. I swear it! You have to believe me. Why would I want to hurt myself? I want to live. I want to be out of this place. I want to be with our daughter, with you." She looked at Colt as she said the last word, her eyes begging him to believe her. He looked down, breaking eye contact. "Colt—" she said, staring at him intently.

"Jenna," Natalie said, stealing her focus. "You know that we love you."

"Of course, I know that. But, look, just take me home already, okay? I'll be better. I *am* better. I'm healing. Please, I want to go home," Jenna pleaded with them.

Colt met her eyes then, tears flooding his own. "Couldn't we just take her home?" he asked finally, glancing at the doctor and then at Natalie.

Natalie shook her head. "It isn't safe for her. You know that. Not yet, anyway. We don't know what she could do. It's not worth the risk, Colt. No matter how badly we *both* want it."

The doctor nodded. "It is ultimately up to you at this point, Mr. Ray. We've held her for twenty-four hours with no further incident. She is under no obligation to stay, but should you choose to keep her under our care, she may need to be transferred to a more permanent facility. She will also need to start therapy twice a week, with me."

"I'm her therapist," Natalie said, her tone fiery. "She isn't ready to be released."

"Actually, Mrs. Pearman, you can't be her therapist while she is in my care, as you well know. And, more to the point, it is neither safe nor practical for her therapist to also be her sister. I personally believe that you acting as her therapist has contributed immensely to what little progress she's made over the years. Had she been working with someone else, I believe she could've made vast improvements."

"Years?" Jenna asked.

"I beg your pardon, Doctor, but she has made great progress under my care. Her case is a complicated one. You couldn't possibly know what we've been through," Natalie replied heatedly.

"Progress? If anything she's gotten worse! Do you really think seeing someone different would help?" Colt asked the doctor.

"Yes, I most certainly do," he answered firmly.

"No," Natalie said at the same time.

"How can you be sure?" Colt asked. Jenna wasn't sure who his question was directed toward. Her head pounded more and more with each question as tension filled the room.

"Colt, look, you can't listen to him. This is just another

case to him. No one knows Jenna's case like I do," Natalie said.

"Which is exactly why she shouldn't be seeing you. You're too close to her," the doctor snapped.

"She's my sister! I want what's best for her. I wouldn't be doing this if I didn't."

"You are not what is best for her. You can't be," the doctor said, looking back to Colt. "I'm sorry, but letting her sister treat her goes against everything I believe in. Everything I've been taught. I really think if—"

"Stop it!" Jenna shrieked, holding her head in pain. "Stop it! All of you! Stop talking about me like I'm not here. I'm sitting right here." The room fell silent, all eyes on her. She felt the burn of frustration on her cheeks, batting back tears of anger. She looked directly at Colt then, her eyes locked with his. "I want to go home." She pressed each word out of her mouth with force.

"Okay," he said finally, exhaling a sigh. "Okay." Natalie looked at him as though he'd betrayed her, not bothering to look at Jenna, yet she said nothing.

"Okay then," the doctor broke the silence. "Let's get you out of here."

---

JENNA SAT in the back seat of the car, her arms wrapped around her daughter in her carseat.

"How is it possible that you have grown so much?" She kissed her head for what seemed like the hundredth time.

"You've been gone, Jenna," Colt said softly, reaching back and rubbing her knee.

"I know," she answered defensively. "But that doesn't make this make any more sense."

"I know it doesn't." He frowned. "Nothing will."

"Did you have fun at Grandma's house?" Jenna asked. Tiffany nodded sleepily. "Your mother has been through so much. Please thank her for me," Jenna told Colt. "I can't imagine how hard it has been on her—losing your father, and now dealing with all of my problems."

"It's been hard on everyone," he said. "You included." Jenna stared at him through the rearview mirror as they pulled in the driveway, his hand leaving her knee. They parked and he shut off the car, climbing out. She unbuckled Tiffany and Colt lifted her out of the carseat in one swift motion. She laid her head on his shoulder instantly, beginning to doze off.

"Someone's had a long day," he whispered, casting a smile toward Jenna. She wrapped an arm around his waist, taking a deep breath as they walked into the house. "I'm going to go put her down," he said.

"No," she said, stopping him and holding her arms out. "Let me." He gently placed Tiffany into her mother's waiting arms, nodding, and kissed both of their foreheads softly.

"Goodnight, princess," he whispered to the girl before looking up at Jenna. "I'll start supper. You must be starving." She nodded, careful not to speak, for fear of waking up their daughter. She turned, walking down the long hallway, noticing the absence of all of their family pictures that had once adorned the walls. The house looked bare without them.

She entered Tiffany's room, placing her down in the small bed gently. She kissed her forehead, brushing her ebony hair away from her face. It took her breath away how beautiful her daughter was, a wave of tears filling her eyes. *How could she have ever left this little girl? What kind of a person does that? What kind of a mother?* Brushing the tears away as she felt them coming on, she pulled the girl's clothes off, slipping her pajamas over her head. Tiffany opened her eyes slightly but was back asleep in an instant, finding comfort in her mother's arms.

After she was dressed and bundled up into a blanket, Jenna turned, shutting off the light and leaving her daughter's room. She made her way toward their bedroom, running her fingers along the white popcorn walls slowly, she wanted to take in every minute of this night. She flicked on the light, staring into a bedroom she hardly recognized. The pictures were missing, the comforter was new, and the mirror that had once hung on the far wall was gone. She sucked in a breath, wondering if she'd done this, if she'd forgotten about it somehow. She walked into the closet, shocked to see most of Colt's clothes missing, a small suitcase lay open on the floor, displaying his clothes. *He was leaving her.* The realization smacked her square in the chest.

She burst out of the room, rushing toward the kitchen in a panic. Colt hurried out of the room to meet her. He grasped her shoulders, letting her cry in his arms.

"What's wrong? What happened? Is Tiffany okay?" he asked.

"Are you leaving me?" she asked, sobs pouring out of her. She couldn't blame him, not really, but it tore her heart up nonetheless.

"Leaving you?" He pulled her away from him, staring at her in confusion. "Jenna, I could never leave you. Would never. Why would you say that?"

She choked back her tears, wiping her eyes to no avail.

"Because I'm crazy. Because you are packing your suitcase. And, I mean, who could blame you, because—"

He kissed her lips firmly, for the first time in what seemed like forever. Their mouths fit together perfectly, like two puzzle pieces side by side. When he pulled away from her, he frowned. "I could never, *would never,* leave you. I'm as in love with you as the day we met and the day we got married. My suitcase is only packed because on the day you left us, you asked me to move out. I respected your wishes. This is still my home. It always has been. I just had to wait until I was welcome again. Until you were ready for me."

The words hit her hard. "I made you...I made you leave? How could I? Why would I?" She covered her eyes and let out a moan. "Oh my god, I'm a monster. Why would you come back?"

"This is my home, Jenna. You are my home. In sickness and in health." He kissed her again, pulling her chin to his.

"It must have been awful," she said, talking in a breath between sobs as she pulled away.

"Yeah. It was. It is," he confirmed.

"How many times has it happened? How many times have I left?" she asked.

He frowned at her. "I don't know."

"That many?"

"We don't have to talk about it. You're here now. That's what matters. I'm so happy to have you back. Come on, let's just eat dinner." He urgently tried to change the subject.

"Colt, I love you for this. For making me feel like any of this is normal. But, it's not. I'm not. And I need to know. I have to learn about it so that I can make it stop somehow," she said.

"I don't think that's a good idea, Jenna. Natalie says it could upset you more to talk about it."

"I just don't know if it could be any worse than not knowing," she said.

He thought for a moment, his eyes dancing between hers. "Okay. What do you want to know?" He sighed out loud, leading her to the couch to sit down.

"What am I like? When it happens, I mean. How do I act?"

He sat down beside her. "You're not...you. When it happens, you're just gone. Jenna is gone."

"What does that mean? I don't understand."

"You—" He bit his lip. "Natalie calls it dissociating. You dissociate into a woman named Monroe."

"Monroe?" she asked, feeling a hint of familiarity deep down inside of her chest.

"Yes, Monroe. Monroe is an old woman, Jenna. Somehow, I don't know how it's even

possible, but Natalie says you believe you're several decades older than you are now. Monroe never had kids. We never had kids."

"We?" she asked.

"Yes. We. I'm still your husband. Monroe's husband. It's the only thing that stays the same between both worlds."

"But...why? Why is that?"

"I don't know. We can't figure it out, honestly. Natalie says it shouldn't be that way."

"Am I...mean to you? Is she?"

He grinned. "Only if I piss her off." She didn't smile. *Couldn't smile.*

"Do you love me when I'm that way? Do you want to leave me because I'm her?" She looked down, preparing herself for any answer.

"I love you in any state, Jenna. And you love me. Our love overpowers everything else."

She looked back up at him, smiling sadly. "Does Natalie know what causes me to act this way?"

"No." He shook his head. "If we knew your trigger, we could try to avoid it, but it's always something different. I never know when it's coming."

"Well, isn't there a medicine I could take? Something to help? Maybe the doctor was right. I mean, maybe I should see someone else, besides Natalie."

"Maybe." He frowned, rubbing her hand. He stood up, walking to look out the door. "Natalie thinks it's a bad idea, though."

"But why?"

"You're...you're very fragile, Jenna. We want to protect you. We just aren't always sure the best way to do that." She started crying again at his words, tears flowing freely. "What is it?" he asked her. "What's wrong?" He rushed back toward her, holding her close to him.

"Am I even worth protecting?" she asked, an overwhelming sense of hopelessness filling her.

"Don't say that," he said. "Don't you dare say that, Jenna. Don't even think it. You have always been and will always be worth everything we do for you."

Without warning, the smoke alarm began going off, interrupting their conversation and causing them both to jump. He rushed toward the kitchen, fanning his hands hurriedly. She followed him. He grabbed a towel from the counter, waving it the air.

"See?" she screamed over the chaos. "This is what I mean. This...all of this, it's all my fault. I just keep screwing everything up."

"No!" he said, fanning the alarm desperately. "It's not your fault, Jenna. None of this is your fault." As the smoke alarm finally stopped, Colt opened the stove, smoke tunneling out. He waved his arm through it, coughing. "Well, off subject and completely unrelated, chicken is not happening. What else would you like?" He turned to her, a small smile on his face.

She sighed, sinking down in a kitchen chair. "I'm not hungry anymore."

"You need to eat, Jenna."

"I just need some water right now," she said, rubbing her forehead.

He grabbed a glass from the cabinet, filling it quickly. "Did the smoke get to you? Are you okay? Should we go back to the hospital?"

"No," she answered, perhaps a bit too quickly. That was the absolute last place she wanted to be. "No. I'm fine, just a bit light headed."

He turned off the tap, walking toward her and handing over the glass before sitting down across from her. The smell of burnt chicken filled the kitchen but it was the last thing on her mind. In the distance, Tiffany began crying.

"The smoke alarm must've woken her up," Colt said, standing up. "I'll be right back."

She nodded, taking a drink of her water. She stared down at her hands, laying her head on the table. Her head was heavy, mind buzzing with questions, and she knew if she lay there for long, she'd be asleep.

Within a few minutes, Tiffany's crying had calmed and Colt reappeared. "You okay?" he asked, putting a hand on her back as he sat down.

"Colt?" she asked, her eyes meeting his.

"Yes?"

"I need you to tell me everything. Every time. I need to know it all."

He sighed, rubbing his temple. "You don't need to put yourself through that."

"Yes. Yes I do. More than anything I do."

"Why? Do you really think it will help?" He shook his head, obviously not wanting to discuss what she was asking from him.

"Right now," she said as she took another sip of water, her hands shaking. "I believe it's the only thing that may help."

"I don't know, Jenna. Natalie says it could make things worse."

"She's wrong, Colt." She took his hands in hers. "Don't you see? This isn't something you two can protect me from. I know you want to but you just can't. The only way to help me is for you to let me help myself. I can't do that unless I know the truth about everything that is going on." She paused, leaning forward and kissing him on the cheek. He kissed her lips softly in return. "I know you want to protect me. And god knows I love you for it, but you aren't protecting me by keeping me in the dark. It doesn't work. You said it yourself, I'm getting worse. Please, Colt. Please just help me." Tears poured from her eyes as she begged her husband for something she knew would destroy her. Her cheeks burned, red and raw, from the salt in her ever flowing tears.

Finally, he exhaled, rubbing her cheek with his thumb. "Okay. But if it gets to be too much, you have to let me know."

"Okay," she agreed. "I will."

And then he told her everything. Every time she'd left. Every time she'd disappeared. Every time he'd met Monroe.

Detail after detail poured out of him: things she couldn't remember, nights that had been long lost to her. She found herself listening with a devouring hunger, desperate to learn and remember every detail that he shared. She needed to learn everything there was to know about Monroe.

# JENNA

Jenna found herself in the woods again. This time, however, her memory was perfectly intact. After Colt had fallen asleep, she'd snuck to the car and driven away from their house without his knowledge. Even after the long talk they'd had, something still didn't sit right with her and she was determined to figure it out. Everything Colt had told her, horrible and terrifying as it may have been, was as if he were reading to her from a book. She couldn't remember a single thing about her dissociative self, Monroe. One thing she remembered with great certainty, though, was waking up only a few mornings ago in a house with her sister. It was a memory Natalie had denied outright, yet she remembered it as clearly as she could remember her talk with Colt only hours ago. It was real. It had happened—of that, she was sure. Her sister was hiding something and she was going to figure out what it was.

She drove to the spot where Colt had picked her up days ago, where the kind man had saved her life. She pulled over on the side of the interstate as she found the small, gravel filled area where David had parked. She shut the car off, looking into the dark woods. She was relying solely on her memory for this part, the memory they'd sworn couldn't be right. She climbed out of the car, pressing the lock button and seeing her headlights blink twice. She pushed the keys into the back pocket of her jeans and started her trek into the woods. She'd come from the right that morning, she remembered, and straight on ahead from there. The woods were pitch black around her, silent and eerie. She kept her breathing quiet though her pulse raced rapidly. The cool, damp leaves were slippery under her feet and she nearly fell a few times. She held on to the trees as she walked, fumbling her way through a woods she couldn't see through.

Though she was frightened at every minuscule sound she heard, she didn't dare pull out her phone to use it for light, in fear it would alert someone to her presence. She wasn't sure why she was so afraid, besides a few animals she doubted there'd be anything or anyone in the woods this late. They'd have no reason to be. Still, her heart jumped at each and every noise she heard.

She walked for what seemed like miles, much longer than the last time, listening carefully for anyone around. When she finally laid eyes on a house in the distance, its porch light was on, as if they were waiting for her. She could see a tower of smoke rising from its chimney through the trees. It was the house she remembered. *She remembered.* A small smile crept onto her face, feeling triumphant. She'd been right all along. She continued to make her way toward the house, Natalie's warning suddenly in her ears. *Run,* she'd told her. *Run and don't ever come back.*

Continuing on, she pushed the warning out of her mind. Just as she had, she gasped, stopping in her tracks. Natalie's car sat in the driveway. *She had lied.* She'd been there that morning after all, and yet she'd made Jenna out to be a liar—let Colt believe she was crazy. Let Jenna believe it herself.

Interrupting her thoughts, she cried out as a branch smacked her arm, ripping her stitches open slightly. She pulled her sleeve down, pressing her palm onto the wound. Blood pooled around the cut, soaking into her shirt. She couldn't stop. Not now. She was far too close to getting the answers she'd been waiting for. She reached the edge of the woods quickly, before she'd realized she was there and she was suddenly standing in the yard, entirely exposed.

The yard had a long circle drive, a tall pine tree in the center. It was beautiful in a rustic way, surrounded by miles of woods with a small pond off to the right. She made her way up the long driveway, the gravel and pinecones crunching under her shoes. A light flashed on from the top of the garage and she froze, fearing her cover had been blown.

She held up her hand, shielding her eyes so that she could see. An older woman stood on the front porch, a tattered flannel robe tied around her. Her wild, graying hair stood on end in every direction and her face was dark and filled with deep wrinkles. Panic engulfed Jenna's organs, turning her insides ice cold.

"What are you doing here?" the woman called out to her, her voice cutting through the silent night.

"I'm...um, I'm looking for Natalie," Jenna called, trying to get a good look at the woman. She looked strangely familiar, but she couldn't see enough of her face to decide why. "My name is Jenna. Jenna Ray. Do you know Natalie?"

"What business is that of yours, Jenna Ray? I could've shot you, you know. I still could. Self-defense and all. You can't just show up on my property in the middle of the night."

Ignoring her heart that continued to pound in her chest, she went on. "I know. I'm really sorry, I know it's late. It's just really important that I find Natalie. Is she here?"

The woman was silent for a moment, her arms remained folded across her body. "Yeah," she said finally. "Yeah, she's here."

"Could I see her?" She took a step forward on instinct.

"Yeah, you can. But, you'll have to come inside." The woman dropped her arms, pulling open the screen door on her porch. "You're costing me money, making me lose all my heat. I don't know where you live, Jenna Ray, but money don't grow on trees around here."

"Of course." Jenna hurried up onto the front porch, following the woman into her house. She looked around the living room. It was quaint, a small fireplace in the corner, two leather sofas and a recliner filling the room. She turned to face the woman, hoping to get a good look at her, but she was facing away, shutting the door.

"Do you want some tea?" the woman asked, her back still turned to Jenna. The light from the fireplace was the only source of light in the small house, giving everything an eerie glow.

"Oh, no thank you. If I could just talk to Natalie, I'll be on my way."

"When someone offers you tea, you take a drink of tea, you brat," the woman hissed at her.

Before Jenna could respond, the woman was out of the room, hurrying toward the kitchen. Her words had chilled Jenna to the bone, filling her with recognition. At that exact moment, Jenna realized what was happening, who the woman was, and exactly why Natalie had warned her never to come back to this house.

She followed the woman into the kitchen, not sure she could believe it. “Momma?”

# JENNA

Her mother turned, her face illuminated by the little bit of light that came from above the kitchen stove. Jenna flipped on a light switch, brightening up the room. She took in a sharp breath, covering her mouth, as she stared into the eyes of a woman who she hadn't seen in years, a woman who had disappeared so long ago.

"What the hell is going on? You...you're supposed to be—"

"Dead?" The woman cackled. "Yeah, well...guess what? I'm not."

"But, how?" Jenna asked, her whole body trembling in fear, anger, and disbelief.

"Life's funny, isn't it?" she asked, turning back to her tea kettle. She poured two cups, one for herself, and the other she handed to Jenna. Jenna stared at the red mug in her trembling hands. It was all coming back to her then: everything that had happened as Monroe, her mother and Natalie drugging her and tying her up here. And just like that, the reason for all of this was there, too. She remembered the night she'd been attacked. The first time. Natalie's boyfriend.

She remembered Dustin, the man her sister had married. The mug fell from her hands, bursting into shards of glass that littered the floor. A brown puddle of tea spread across the white tile.

"Now, what'd you go and do that for?" the woman asked, staring at her daughter with pure hatred in her eyes.

"How...could...you?" Jenna asked, her bottom lip quivering as she held back anger-filled tears.

"How could I what? Pour you a glass of tea? Yes, how dare I?" The woman stared at her daughter and then at the mess on the floor but didn't dare move.

*"How could you?"* Jenna demanded. "I was just a child. I was just a distraught, terrified little girl and you lied to me. I needed you to protect me. To tell me that everything was okay. I needed you to be my mother and instead you just...you lied to me. You made me feel like this was all my fault. All these years—" She trailed off, wiping a stray tear that ran down her cheek.

Her mother didn't move, her face expressionless. "It *was* all your fault, you stupid, stupid girl. You were leading that boy on from the second he walked into our house that night. I told you that you needed to go to bed, Jenna. I tried to get you to go to bed, but you refused. You never listened. No, you always thought you knew best, you were...stubborn. Always so stubborn, and headstrong, *and stupid.* You were too stupid for your own good, Jenna, and it's about time you heard that."

"I was just a child! I didn't know any better. I had no idea what he was capable of. How dare you act like my stubbornness justifies what he did? You were supposed to protect me. That was your job as my mother." She took a step back from her, trying to catch her breath.

"And what should I have done, Jenna? Put you in court? Let you testify against him? Ruin your life? Because that's exactly what would have happened if we'd done anything. If I'd let you go to the police, let you go to court, all anyone would have talked about when your name came up was that you were a *victim,* Jenna. Is that what you wanted? To be a victim? You were better than that. We are better than that. Our friends, our neighbors...the awful things they would've said about you, about us. You can't possibly understand the decision I had to make or why I did the things I did."

"The things you did? Are you kidding me right now? You ruined my life by doing absolutely nothing. You didn't even try. You let me feel, every single day, that I had done something wrong, that I should be ashamed of what happened."

Her mother placed her palm under her cup, walking toward the large window at the end of the kitchen. She stared outside for a few moments before speaking again, Jenna couldn't see her face.

"You forgot what happened, Jenna. You weren't in any pain. You weren't suffering. As long as we kept Dustin away from you, as long as we made sure he never came into contact with you, you just...forgot. I hurt no one with my decision."

The gravity of the situation pounded in her chest, her head spinning. She looked down at the puddle growing cold around her feet before glancing back up.

"My sister married the man who raped me," she said the sentence quietly, then repeated it again a bit louder. Finally, she screamed it, looking at her mother, silently begging her to turn around and meet her eyes. Heat rose throughout her body, her anger burning her skin.

Her mother turned around, staring at her calmly. "Now,

you just hush, Jenna. Quit all of that screaming. Your sister's husband is a good man. Sure, he's made some mistakes, but he is good to us. He makes great money and uses that money to take care of this family. He's done more for me over the years than you ever have. You have no idea what sort of pressure he was under when he—" she paused, seeming to search for the word Jenna knew she was refusing to use.

"*Raped me*? Say the word, Mother. Avoiding it doesn't make it any less real."

"Made his unfortunate mistake," her mother corrected.

"It wasn't a mistake, Mother. It was a crime! How can you make excuses for him? How can you stand there and take up for him to my face?"

"He was just a kid, Jenna!" She slammed her mug down onto the kitchen table, tea flying everywhere. It sloshed out onto her hand, scalding her skin. She cursed, covering her hand with her mouth and rushing to the sink. She turned the faucet on, placing the wound under it and sighing before looking over her shoulder at her daughter. "See what you did, you stupid girl. You were always so pitiful. Never taking responsibility for anything. It was always someone else's fault."

"You hateful, hateful woman," Jenna spat out, stepping over the puddle of tea finally and walking toward her mother. She wasn't sure what she was going to do, only that her rage was growing out of control with each word her mother spoke. "You say these things to make yourself feel better about what a shit job you did as a parent."

The woman turned to her, revulsion in her eyes. She swung her arm hard, smacking her daughter in the face with a loud THWACK. "Don't you ever, ever speak to me that way again! Do you hear me? You're the one who came here, you're the one who found me. I will not have you in my house speaking to me like that."

Jenna clutched her face in shock, rubbing her cheek. She put her hand down, unwilling to allow her mother to see her pain. She felt the heat growing in the place where she was sure a handprint must be. "*I* found *you?* This time, maybe. But only after you brought me here. Only after you tied me up and drugged me and kept me prisoner. I thought you were dead! I came here tonight looking for Natalie, not you."

"I certainly did not tie you up or drug you. That was all your sister's doing. Not me. You weren't worth the trouble to me. I wanted you out of the picture years ago. It would've saved everybody a lot of trouble."

She gulped, reeling back as if she'd been slapped again. She clutched her chest. "You wanted to...to what—*kill me*? You wanted me dead? I was that much of a nuisance to you? That you'd kill your own daughter?"

Her mother sighed as if she were being dramatic, turning to shut off the faucet. "I wanted you to leave us all alone, Jenna. I just wanted you to leave us in peace. But you wouldn't. You would never let it go, what happened. You would never just...just *drop it.* It was Natalie who wanted to work with you. She wanted to make sure that you forgot so that you could go on with your life and we could go on with ours." She took a deep breath, rubbing her forehead. "But you never forgot, Jenna. You wouldn't."

"Do you hear yourself right now? Do you even understand how crazy you sound?"

The woman looked at her with wild eyes. "Crazy? Do you even understand what it's like to live the life we do because of that man? The man who *ruined your life.*" She made air quotations around the words. "Grow up, Jenna. That man provides for us. He gives your sister and I a good life. That's all we've ever wanted. He's the CEO of a marketing agency." She said the words as if she were announcing that he was the President of the United States. "Big money, Jenna. Life changing money. We have to keep him happy or all of that stops. Don't you see that?"

There was something small there in her eyes that Jenna saw, the hint of what looked similar to an apology.

"He's still doing it," she said, trying to plead with any piece of humanity still inside of her mother. "He's still hurting me. It wasn't just the one time. He's done it so many times since then. He could be hurting other women, other girls." She waited for her mother to respond. When she didn't, she asked, "Did you know that?" She continued to stare at her, no words coming out of her mouth. Her lack of denial was a confirmation. If she hadn't known, she still didn't care.

"Does Natalie know?"

Again, the woman said nothing, her lips pressed together tightly.

"But, why fake your own death? Why disappear? I don't understand. What good did that do?" She walked back to the table, grabbing a towel off the back of a chair and mopping up the tea that had spilled, still ignoring the growing puddle on the floor. "Dustin suggested that. It was a way to get you to leave us all alone. Every time you saw me, it brought back your memories. The ones we'd worked so hard to get you to forget. We knew, in order for you to remain ignorant, I would have to stay away from you. It was no problem for me, trust me, but you just wouldn't leave me alone. And after you told your counselor in high school that something had happened to you, the school called me and wanted to talk.

They were worried about you and I think a little suspicious of me. It was Dustin who helped to keep things calm, to get their eyes off of me. But we knew, at that point, that something had to be done."

"I just...I don't get it."

"What is there to get?"

"I don't understand how you can choose money over your daughter's life." She stared at her mother, disgust in her eyes. How was it possible to truly not recognize the evil in someone? How had the same woman who'd taught her how to color and taken her school shopping have had this darkness in her all along?

"Oh, Jenna, you aren't dead. Don't be dramatic." The insensitivity in her voice stung and Jenna was brought back to the night it happened, to her mother's emptiness when she'd needed her the most.

"I'm not dead? *I feel dead*, mother. Every single day. I feel dead. And I never understood why. Never. But you knew. All this time. All this time you and Natalie and that...*that monster*, you knew. You could've helped me, you could've saved me but instead you just chose to let me keep living with it. You chose to let me keep feeling so horribly empty and not knowing, not remembering, why. Colt told me that I've gone missing for days, weeks, on end. I come home starving, dehydrated, and filthy. I forget my name, I forget who I am, I forget my age, my daughter. So, while, yes, in the very literal sense, I am not dead, most days I might as well be. That, all of that, is on you. That's your fault and yet you sit here, staring at me, with this look on your face that tells me you don't care. How is that possible? What kind of a mother does that?" Tears filled her eyes again, her vision blurring, but this time she refused to wipe them away.

"I don't know, Jenna. I don't know what kind of a mother all of this makes me. But let me ask you this: you forget your own daughter. What kind of a mother does *that*?" the woman asked smugly, a cruel smile on her face.

Something in her snapped in that moment, fury unlike anything she'd felt before rose up from her gut. She smacked her mother in the face, feeling the bones in her hand connect with her jawline. Her head swung back on contact. The sting in Jenna's hand spread throughout her palm.

Her mother covered her cheek, looking at her daughter in disbelief. "Why you little—" She approached her with vengeance, her arm raised, ready to exact her revenge. Acting on instinct, Jenna leapt forward, shoving her back. She didn't think twice as the woman tumbled back, her eyes full of fear. She slipped on the puddle of Jenna's spilled tea, her feet flailing under her. She fell to the floor, her head hitting the tile with a sickening crunch.

Jenna took a deep breath, realizing what she'd done. It wasn't supposed to go this way. She knew that as she stared down at the mess she had made. The thick, dark blood pooled over the white tile of her mother's kitchen, mixing with the puddle of already cold tea. Her body lay in front of her, skull so instantly thick with blood that she could hardly see the wound where the blood was pouring out. Head wounds bled a lot. She'd always heard that. But, this was unlike anything she'd ever seen. There was just *so* much. Her whole body shook with fear and adrenaline, throat tight.

She would never forget the way the cracking of her skull had echoed through the empty house or the look on her face as she slammed onto the floor. The panic was plastered there, even now, her mouth gaped open, eyes, even in death, filled with terror.

It was over. Just like that. She was gone. Her mother was dead. She stepped over a trail of blood as it made its way toward her. The blood was quickly spreading everywhere she looked. It was hard to believe her tiny body had even held so much blood. She had to get out of there. She tried to remember, quickly, any place she had touched as she walked through the house, wiping away possible fingerprints as she went.

When she was sure she'd wiped away any trace of evidence that she'd ever been there, she darted out the door, running from the house, and racing toward the woods as fast as her legs would carry her. Natalie's car still remained in the driveway and as she ran she expected someone to jump out and stop her. *Try to stop her*. Natalie, Dustin, someone. But no one did. The dark of the night swallowed her up, concealing her guilty getaway. She panted, her whole body burning, but she refused to quit moving. Her arm dripped blood which she tried to keep covered up. Her stitches would have to be sewn up again. She hit the edge of the woods quickly, darting through the trees and disappearing into the darkness.

## JENNA

Just as Jenna made it to the edge of the woods, she heard her name. A voice whispered softly, calling out to her. "Jenna?"

She spun around quickly, ready to attack. "Natalie?"

Her sister stood just behind her, only the light of dawn on her face. She stared at her, her face full of horror. "Jenna? What did you do?"

"What are you talking about?" Jenna asked, voice full of denial.

"I know you found the house, found Momma. I saw you leave, saw you running away. What happened? Why were you there?"

Just like that, the wall in her shattered. She tried to catch her breath, but the sadness and anger that filled her took it away again. "How could you? How could you keep this from me? You lied to me. All of this time, you were lying to me. All of this time. I trusted you! I believed all of your lies. I counted on you. How could I have been so dumb?"

"No, Jenna." She tried to approach her, her hands held out

for her sister. Jenna leapt back, her arms up for protection. "Jenna, I didn't have a choice. Don't you see that? I only wanted to protect you. Everything I ever did was to protect you."

"No!" Jenna screamed. "No. That's a lie. You didn't protect me, Nat. You lied to me. You protected *him*." Her sister's voice caught in her throat, tears could be heard on her breath but Jenna went on. "You protected him all these years. You kept me close to make sure I wouldn't tell anyone what he did. What you all did."

"Jenna—"

"No!" Jenna screamed again, taking another step back.

"I never wanted it to be like this. I swear to you, I didn't. I didn't even know what happened in the beginning."

"Momma told me everything, Natalie. So, you can save whatever speech you have prepared. I don't trust you anymore."

"I *didn't know*. Not in the beginning. You have every right to be furious with me. To hate me. To never trust me again. I don't blame you, Jenna. I could never blame you. But, I didn't want any of this to hurt you, and believe it or not, I've done all of this to protect you. I got my degree solely to be able to help you. Every day I've worked to keep you safe. Not him. You. My allegiance has always been to you, Jenna, never him."

Jenna paused. "How? How was any of this protecting me?"

"When I found out what he'd done to you, it was because I walked in on Momma and Dustin talking about it. It was *over a year* after it happened. I was furious. I hated him. I hated her. I wanted to help you. I wanted to turn him in. I was ready to go to the police right then, I swear to you I was, but I couldn't. She is our mother, Jenna."

"And I'm your sister."

"Yes. Yes, you are my sister. And I should've done right by you. Of course I should have. I made a mistake. I listened to her. I believed her when she said that we were doing what was best for all of us. You included. She convinced me that she was doing what she could to protect you, too."

"That's a lie. She never cared about protecting me. She told me she wanted me dead."

Natalie was quiet for a moment. When she spoke again, her voice was softer, calm somehow. "I didn't see that side of our mother until it was too late. I'd already helped you to keep those memories blocked out. By the time I realized how evil our mother was, you'd already forgotten. You had peace for the first time in longer than I could know. I couldn't ask you to lose that. I couldn't stand to see you hurt, Jen."

"You know, I have to admit. You're pretty good at this whole lying thing. Then again, I guess all of the practice over the years has you at a slight advantage."

"Stop it. Just, just please hear me out. What I did, Jenna, what I did was despicable. I know that. I have to live with my choices, my decisions, every single day. When you started becoming Monroe, I honestly did want to bring you back. I wanted my little sister back, no matter the cost. Even if that meant all of us going to jail. It destroyed me to watch how badly this had affected you, you have no idea how that felt—to have to watch what you'd become, what we'd let you become. I wanted to protect you then even though the thought of what could happen to us terrified me."

When Jenna didn't respond, Natalie continued. "But every time I tried, every theory I had, just made you dissociate more. I brought Dustin around you, I mentioned Tiffany in your pictures, I even had you go to Colt's apartment to see her. I wanted my sister back. I missed you so much. And I was going to tell you. I honestly was. No matter what it cost me, I was going to tell you the truth. But then, Dustin did it again." She burst into sobs, her whole body shaking.

"He never stopped hurting me, Natalie. Did you realize that? Never. I have all of these memories. They keep coming back to me." Jenna said the words slowly, watching her sister hurt over them. "Your husband is a monster."

"I know," she said through her tears. "I know that. I mean, I didn't know it. Not until the night you went to the hospital. Well, okay, I suspected it. After I saw the bruises. I begged you to tell me the truth. I decided, if you would admit it, if you would tell me what he'd done, I'd turn him in myself. But you wouldn't."

"I couldn't. My brain is so *damn* screwed up because of what you all have done that I couldn't remember what happened. I honestly thought I'd just slipped. Little dumb Jenna fell down again. More bruises for little dumb Jenna."

"The night that you went to the hospital, Mom convinced me that I had to bring you back to our house."

"You mean kidnap me."

"I listened to her. I don't know why. After all of this time, it's like she has some sort of hold over me. I was never going to hurt you, Jenna. I wouldn't. I kept you safe. Mom and Dustin, they wanted you gone a long time ago. I wouldn't let them hurt you."

"What do you want, Natalie? A medal? An award? *Congratulations for not killing me?*"

"I want you to know the truth."

"So, what? So, you didn't kill me. You didn't physically hurt me. That doesn't make you a saint in all of this."

"Of course not."

"So, you should just go. Before I get to the police. Because this time I'm telling them the truth, Natalie. This time I'm turning you all in. Unless you want to kill me now."

"I would never hurt you, Jenna."

"So, what? I shouldn't hurt you because you didn't hurt me?"

"That's not what I'm saying." Her sobs echoed through the forest.

"Stop crying, Natalie. Just stop it. It won't change my mind."

"I don't want to change your mind, Jenna. You should turn me in. You should turn all of us in. But before you do, there's one more thing you should know."

"What? What more could there possibly be?"

"You're going to die."

# COLT

Colt woke up the next morning from one of the greatest nights of sleep he'd had in a long time. He yawned, stretching out across the bed. As he leaned over, his eyes still blurry from sleep, and reached for his wife, his heart plummeted. Jenna was gone.

"Jenna?" He sat up in their bed, looking around the room. "Jenna, where are you?" He leapt up from bed, immediately going into action. He'd been here too many times before.

He walked around their bedroom, searching in the closet and in dresser drawers where he knew she couldn't hide. It was as if his wife had become a figment of his own imagination and there were endless possibilities for hiding places anymore.

When he realized she wasn't in their bedroom, he ventured out into the rest of the house, throwing a shirt over his head. "Jenna?" he called into the quiet house.

"Daddy?" He heard Tiffany say his name from down the hallway. She stood in her bedroom door, rubbing sleep from her eyes.

"Hey, Tiff." He tried to blink away the tears that had already begun forming in his eyes. He'd known he should've never told Jenna everything he told her last night. It was too much for her to handle, Natalie had warned him of that. He walked to his daughter, scooping her up. "Good morning, sunshine."

"What's wrong, Daddy?" she asked him, touching a tear with her fingertip. He wiped it away quickly, kissing her cheek.

"Nothing's wrong, Tiff. Let's go into the living room and turn on some cartoons. How does that sound?"

"Yeah!" she screamed excitedly, clapping her hands.

He walked into the living room, his eyes searching wildly for his wife, when he felt his heart stop suddenly. He stared into the kitchen—there, taped to the countertop was a piece of paper from a yellow, legal pad. His knees grew weak as he wondered what it might be, deep down knowing it couldn't be good. He set Tiffany down on the living room floor, not bothering to turn on the TV, his gaze locked onto the note. He could think of nothing else.

Tiffany, immediately realizing that he hadn't turned on her cartoons, followed him into the kitchen, tugging on his pant leg. She was saying his name, yet he couldn't look down at her, his eyes filled with tears now.

He grabbed hold of the note, his hands shaking. His breathing grew quiet as he read the letter, not realizing he was holding his breath. He clasped the paper as if it were Jenna herself, so soft and delicate, careful not to crease or tear it. He wasn't sure if he could bear to read it, fearing what it might say. He heard each word in her voice, her sweet, beautiful voice:

*Dear Colt,*

*I'm sorry, sweetheart, for sneaking off like this. This time isn't like the last. I'm still here, still the Jenna you know. At least, for this moment, I am. I want you to know how much I love you, how much our love means to me. I need so badly for you to believe that our love has saved me, because it has. You have saved me, Colt. You've done so much more for me than I could have ever asked for. You've loved me through the impossible and for that I can never thank you enough.*

*I hope someday you can understand why I had to do this. I need answers, Colt, answers that you can never give me. Natalie has been lying to us, that much I know. What I don't know, is why. I have to know why, my love. I have to know the truth. So much of my life has been masked in lies and I can't bear it anymore.*

*I also, and it breaks my heart to write these words, can't bear to see your heart break one single time more. I have been the cause of so much of your heartache and it hurts me to know just how true that is. If I were a selfish woman, I would stay with you forever, soaking up your love, enjoying every minute with you, loving you for the rest of my life. But for your sake, I can't do that anymore. I am going to love you every day for the rest of my life, how could I ever stop? But I can't be selfish with you anymore, Colt. I can't do that to you or Tiffany.*

*With everything you told me last night, I could see the pain in your eyes as you spoke. I have hurt you, and though I've never meant to, that doesn't make it any less true. You are a good man. You have been an amazing husband and best friend to me. You're more than I could ever ask for or dream of.*

*Please understand that I am doing this for you. I know how much you love me, Colt, but I don't know how much longer I'll be me, or when Monroe will be back. I can't continue to put you through this. To kick you out of your house, to make you take our daughter and leave in the middle of the night, to scream at you, to blame you for leaving me.*

*I just can't do it anymore.*

*You are the best thing that ever happened to me but I am your worst. You deserve better.*

*You deserve to be happy, Colt, and as long as I'm around...that can never be.*

*Be happy, my love. I'll be happy knowing that I've given you that. I'll see you in my dreams. Every night. Take care of our girl.*

*Love always,*

*Jenna*

# JENNA

"Excuse me?" Jenna asked Natalie, shocked by her words.

"I'm the one who cut your wrist with that needle, Jenna. It wasn't you. You never tried to hurt yourself. It was me."

Jenna looked down at her wrist, staring at the bandage in shock. "I knew it. I told you I didn't hurt myself. *I told you*. Why would you do that? Why would you want to hurt me? Has that been your plan all along? What about everything you said?"

"I never wanted to hurt you, Jenna. I meant what I said. I did it so that I could protect you. It was the only way I knew how."

"Protect me? What are you talking about?"

"Momma and Dustin are going to kill you."

"What?"

"That's their plan. After you escaped, they wanted to kill you. Even before that, at the house, they'd said it. They say you're too much of a risk. They are worried about you remembering what happened and then telling the police.

Honestly, I'm surprised you made it out of that house alive. When I found you and you were...well, *you*. I knew I had to save you. I knew your only chance was to get out of that house and as far away from them as possible. That's why I made you leave, why I helped you out the window. That's why I told you to never come back. But, they were still going to go through with it. Once you were home they were going to sneak over and get you again. I don't know that I could've protected you then. And I don't know what they would've done to anyone who tried to stop them." Natalie stared at her sister and Jenna realized what she meant: Colt and Tiffany would've been in danger too.

"I cut your wrist," Natalie went on, "because I thought that would make the doctors decide to hold you for longer. I thought it would keep you safe until I could come up with a plan to get you out of there safely, to get you away from Momma and Dustin for good. I never wanted to hurt you. But they did. They *do,* Jenna. You aren't safe. You won't be safe, not as long as you remain here. Neither will Colt. Or Tiffany. They're in as much danger as you are. Especially if they ever learn the truth. You have to leave. Or be locked up. She can't get to you if you're in the hospital. Or in a ward. I know that's not what you want but—"

"Natalie, Mom's dead."

"W-what?" she asked, taking a step toward her, her eyes blinking rapidly.

"Momma, she can't kill me because she's dead. She can't hurt anyone anymore."

"What are you talking about, Jenna? How would you know that?" She stared at her sister, eyes wide, as it sank in. "No. You couldn't. You wouldn't."

"I didn't mean to," she answered, though for the first time

she realized she wasn't sure if that was completely true. "She came after me. She was going to hurt me, trying to kill me. I did what I had to do, but it was an accident."

Suddenly, a car pulled down the long driveway, its headlights cutting into the woods where they stood. Natalie and Jenna both froze. The sound of their breathing filled the silence as his car tires crunched slowly on the gravel road.

Natalie nodded. "Jenna, you have to go."

"What?"

"It's him," Natalie whispered. The car came to a stop and they heard it shut off. "Natalie?" They heard him yelling their names. His voice sent chills down her spine. "Kim?"

"Go, Jenna! Go! Take Colt and Tiff and get far away from here. None of you are safe. You need a plan and you need one fast. Now that you're you again he wants you dead. He can't risk you telling anyone the truth. He can't ever find you. If he does, I'm not sure I can protect you anymore," she whispered. Jenna nodded, though she didn't move. Natalie approached her, pulling her into a hug. "I know that you'll never forgive me, but I really am sorry. I love you more than you'll ever know. Now, go, baby sis. Get out of here. *Quick*."

Without having to be told again, Jenna ripped herself from her sister's arms. She took off running, her footsteps heavy and loud. She couldn't stand to be quiet any longer, just needing to get out of those woods.

She heard Natalie hollering, her voice covering up any noise that Jenna was making.

"Dustin?" she screamed. "Dustin, it's me."

"What are you doing out here, babe?"

"It's Momma," she said then, the sadness in her voice sounding wholly genuine.

Jenna continued to run, until their voices were so faint

she could hardly hear them and she began to see headlights in the distance. Finally, she allowed herself to stop, crouching down as she tried to catch her breath. She found herself wondering if her sister would truly mourn their mother's death or whether she was faking that too. Could Jenna actually believe anything she'd told her? She realized, then, that she had never truly known her sister, and now, she never would.

# COLT

Colt drove to the hospital in a state of complete panic, his hands shaking on the wheel. His knuckles were pure white as he pulled into the parking lot, his whole body weak and on edge. The police hadn't been able to tell him much when they'd called except that he needed to get there right away.

It had to be Jenna. He knew that much. Her note had left little room for interpretation this morning; she'd gone after Natalie, but he couldn't be sure why. Natalie hadn't answered her phone when he'd tried calling. It didn't feel right, not letting her know what was going on. He wondered if Jenna had found her, maybe she'd already be there with her. Shaking his head, he pushed the thought from his mind. *She would have called.* He checked his phone again, hoping to see that she'd called back but the screen remained empty.

He walked through the hospital's automatic doors and approached the nurses' station. "I'm here to see Jenna Ray," he told them before he'd even been acknowledged. None of the nurses looked up; a receptionist held up her pointer finger, telling him to wait.

After what seemed like an eternity, Colt could wait no longer. He pounded his fists on the counter, the sound filling the quiet hallway. "I need to see my wife!" he bellowed.

The older nurse directly in front of him looked up, a shocked expression on her face.

He held up his hands in surrender. "I'm, look, I'm sorry. I shouldn't have done that. I'm just, I'm panicking a little bit. Can you please just tell me where my wife is? The police called me. Something's happened and I'm very worried about her. Please just give me her room number. Her name's Jenna. Jenna Ray."

The nurse turned without saying a word, grabbing a stack of manila folders. She sifted through them quickly. Eventually, she stopped at one, opening it up. Her eyes danced along the pages, flipping through them.

"Room 208," she said finally without looking up.

"Thank you," he shouted, patting the counter. He dashed away from the nurses' station, running down the halls. He zigzagged in between patients and doctors alike, headed toward the hallway that housed her hospital room. When he finally laid eyes on her room number, darting directly for her door, two police officers approached him. One held out his hand, stopping Colt from entering the room.

"Colt Ray?"

"Yes," he responded, stepping back from the door, and turning toward the officers. He recognized one of the officers who had helped Jenna the last time they'd been here. "I'm here to see my wife, Jenna. Can you tell me what's going on?"

"Yes," the officer said, nodding. "But, let's step over here for a moment. We should talk privately." They led Colt to a bench at the end of the hallway, gesturing for him to have a seat. He did. They stood in front of him, grim looks on their faces.

"Okay, you guys are starting to scare me." He forced a laugh. "Is she okay? She's okay, right?"

The other officer held up his hand, trying to calm him down. "Your wife is fine, Mr. Ray. She's just resting right now. We found her along the highway this morning. She had passed out."

"Passed out? Oh my god."

"Your wife had vomited several times and has fresh cuts on her arms, legs, and face. It was a very similar situation to how we found her the last time. In fact, she was found only about a mile from where we found her before."

"Oh god," Colt said, trying to process everything he was being told. "Okay, you said she was vomiting. Had she been drinking? Could she tell you why she was there? Did something happen to her? Was she attacked again?"

The cop held up his hand again. "Mr. Ray, we know this is all very difficult for you to hear. We need you to stay calm."

Colt nodded, taking a deep breath. The other officer spoke up. "There was no alcohol in Jenna's system. We haven't been able to question her just yet; the doctors have been working to get her stable. We should be able to speak with her soon. Her doctors say there are no signs of any injuries other than those caused by her being in the woods again. That being said, at this time, we don't believe she was attacked. But, of course, we can't be sure of that until we can talk to her further."

"Okay." Colt shook his head in disbelief. "Everything was so good last night. She was, she seemed so present. I can't understand why she would be out there again." He wasn't sure whether or not he should tell the police officers about the letter yet. He wanted to talk to Jenna first.

"Listen," the first officer went on. "I'm afraid there's a bit more you should know. We wanted to talk to you about this before we spoke with her." Colt swallowed hard, bracing himself for the worst.

"The area where we found Jenna, where we'd found her the first time, it wasn't far from a house back in the woods. This morning, when we found Jenna, we weren't just out patrolling that area. We were on our way to that house because—" He sighed, his eyes showing sympathy. "Someone reported a murder there."

"Murder?" His breath caught in his chest as his face fell. "What? I—I don't understand. What are you saying?"

"The call was anonymous, so we don't know yet whether the caller was with Jenna. We don't know anything right now. But when we arrived, we found a woman in the house. We haven't been able to confirm her identity just yet, nor have we been able to contact the homeowner, but, Mr. Ray, it doesn't look good for Jenna."

"What do you mean? You think that Jenna—" he stopped short, waving his hands as if to ward off their suspicions. "No. No. There's no way. You can't possibly believe that Jenna could somehow be involved in this. She wouldn't."

The officers glanced at each other before turning back to Colt. Neither of them spoke, their mouths tight.

"She would never hurt anyone. She couldn't. She's the gentlest person I know. Just, you just have to talk to her to see that. Trust me, you've got this all wrong."

"Mr. Ray, we need to ask you a few questions. We need you to be honest with us, okay? The house was registered to a man named Dustin Pearman. Do you happen to recognize that name?"

He shook his head. "No, but I know the name Pearman. Her sister, Natalie, her last name is Pearman. I've been trying to call her this morning. I haven't been able to get ahold of her. I don't know, maybe they're related." He paused, staring into space for a moment. "Wait a second," he said, his heart seeming to beat hard enough he was sure you could've seen it through his shirt. "You said a woman was murdered. Oh my God...wait, was it, I mean, Natalie? It couldn't be. Jenna wouldn't. I mean, she said Natalie was out there with her. She said she was lying, but even so, she wouldn't. I mean, it's her sister. I can't—" He squeezed his hands onto his knees, trying to catch his breath.

"It wasn't Natalie Pearman," the officer told him, "though we haven't been able to reach her either. Dustin Pearman is, in fact, her husband. This woman, whoever she was, was much older than Mr. or Mrs. Pearman."

The officers exchanged a look that told Colt there was even more bad news. He raised his eyebrows, not sure he could take much more.

"What? What's that look?" he demanded.

"Well." The officer sat down beside him, lowering his voice. "What exactly do you know about the rest of Jenna's family?"

"I don't. I don't know anything about them. Natalie is all that she's got left, besides myself and Tiffany. Her mother passed away a few years ago, before we even met. And her dad was gone before that. He bailed when she was really young. I don't think she even remembers him."

The officer frowned, pulling out his notebook. "Okay. Do you happen to recall either of her parents' names?"

Colt shook his head, rubbing his temple. "Um, no, I don't think so." He thought to himself, trying to remember if Jenna or Natalie had ever mentioned their names. "Wait, Kim, maybe? Kim. I think Kim's right. Kim Jackson. That was her mother's name, I believe. I'm not positive, but I think she's mentioned it before. Or maybe Natalie has. I don't know. That sounds right though. I don't know that she ever knew her father's name."

The officers looked at each other again, their lips tight. Their faces showed a confirmation that Colt was sure couldn't be good news.

"What? What is it? Does this have something to do with her parents?"

The officer sitting beside him sighed, looking back at Colt. "Well, we don't know anything for certain yet. *But*," he emphasized the word, "we found two cars at the house this morning. One in the driveway was registered to Natalie Pearman. That wasn't too much of a surprise, since the house was registered to her husband. The other, however, was registered to a Kimberly Jackson. A woman who we, along with the State of Mississippi, believed to be dead."

"What? What does that mean? Her mother is alive?" His thoughts jumbled up at the new information. Had her mother been alive all along? Did Natalie know this? Where was Natalie and why wouldn't she have answered his calls?

Then, new thoughts filled him. Natalie had claimed to have not known why Jenna was in the woods that morning, yet her car was at a house in the same woods? A house that was registered to her husband. Could that truly be a coincidence? Natalie had never done anything to make him suspect that her intentions toward Jenna were anything but noble, but could he have been wrong? Had he put Jenna into harm's way after all? Even after all of these years, he still knew very little about Natalie except for her relationship with Jenna.

"We aren't sure what it means right now. It could simply mean that the registration was never updated to the new owner," the officer told him. "We really can't say much more until we hear back from the coroner and we officially identify the body. We'll keep you posted as we learn more."

"Thank you."

"You can go and see Jenna now." The officer stood, putting his notebook back into his pocket. The two men walked away, leaving Colt to his thoughts. He wasn't sure he could even move. His head felt so heavy.

After a few minutes, he stood up, walking to her door as he braced himself for the absolute worst. He knocked twice, pressing it open, and looking in to see the woman he loved. He walked into the room in slow motion, still processing everything that had happened to him in this short, yet exhausting, morning.

He was surprised to see that Jenna was awake, lying in the bed. She turned her head when the door opened, her eyes wide in fear. She relaxed when she saw it was him, her whole body seeming at ease. She smiled at him softly.

"Hey," he said quietly.

"Hey," she said.

"How, um, how are you?" he asked.

"I'm okay." She waved him over, taking hold of his hands. "Sore, but okay. I'm so glad that you came."

He nodded, already beginning to cry. He looked her over, studying the scratches and bruises that now covered her body like tattoos, nasty reminders of the horror they had survived the last few days.

"Of course I came, sweetheart. I love you so much."

"I love you too, Colt," she told him, laying her head on his shoulder.

"You scared me this morning," he said, kissing her forehead.

She pulled her head back, staring up at him. "I know." Her voice was filled with sorrow, yet she didn't bother to explain.

"What were you doing out there? Alone? You could've been hurt. You could've been killed. And that note? Please, please don't ever scare me like that again. What were you thinking, Jenna?"

She stared at him, a sadness in her hauntingly beautiful eyes, but she didn't speak. She reached up, grabbing his neck and pulling him down into a kiss. Tears fell from their eyes, meeting and mixing on their cheeks. His heart was full of so many emotions and yet in that moment all he wanted was to be with the woman he'd sworn his life to. It was impossible to imagine his life without her, no matter the cost. She was worth everything she'd put him through.

She pulled back, foreheads pressed together, but their mouths apart. He could feel her breath on his lips. He leaned forward, trying to kiss her again, but she resisted. He opened his eyes, staring at her strangely.

"I'm sorry," she whispered. "I'm so sorry."

"Sorry?" he asked.

She shook her head, her eyes distant now, and his heart sank. He knew her next words before she spoke them, each one like a dagger to his already bruised and beaten heart.

She blinked her eyes, her face filled with pain. "Who's Jenna?"

# STAY UP TO DATE ON EVERYTHING KMOD!

Thank you so much for reading this story. I'd love to invite you to sign up for my mailing list and text alerts so we can be sure you don't miss my next release.

Sign up for my mailing list here:
kierstenmodglinauthor.com/nlsignup

Sign up for my text alerts here:
kierstenmodglinauthor.com/textalerts

# ACKNOWLEDGMENTS

In this crazy, emotional thing we call life, Jenna had Colt by her side, even on her worst days.

I'm so lucky to have my own version of a Colt, whom I love more than words can say: to my husband, Michael. Thank you for supporting my dreams every step of the way and for loving me even when I'm grumpy because my characters won't cooperate— I swear it's not my fault! I'm so grateful we get to share this beautiful life together. You are amazing.

To my daughter, who I dedicated this book to, and who won't be allowed to read it for many, many years. I love you, sweetheart, more than anything else in the world. This book was written through many sleepless nights during your amazing newborn days. So many times I had you bouncing on one knee, while I typed one-handed, but I would do it all again for you. I hope that someday you read mommy's stories and you realize that no matter what your dreams are, they are 100% possible, and I will be there every step of the way supporting you. You are my sunshine.

To my parents: Dennis and Dawn, my sisters: Kaitie, Kortnee, and Kyleigh, and my grandparents: Beth and Chet and Pam and Dennis, thank you for believing in me. Thank you for being there for me every day for my entire life. I'm so thankful to have you crazy people to call my family. You guys made me who I am today and I can never thank you enough.

To my PA: Brittany, for always encouraging me and being support system when no one else understands!

To my Formatter, Lee Ching, thank you for making this book so beautiful. Your work never ceases to amaze me.

To my editor, Sarah, you are the very best! Thank you for all of your insights!

And as always, to each and every one of you who bought this book: thank you. Thank you for continuing to support my dream and thank you for buying my books. I hope that you've enjoyed them so far. Thank you for leaving reviews, lending this book to a friend, or just talking about my work. I appreciate everything you guys do for me. You'll never know what your support has meant. I hope that you'll continue to read my stories and connect with me. I love my readers!

# ABOUT THE AUTHOR

KIERSTEN MODGLIN is an Amazon Top 10 bestselling author of psychological thrillers and a member of International Thriller Writers, Novelists, Inc., and the Alliance of Independent Authors. Kiersten is a KDP Select All-Star and a recipient of *ThrillerFix*'s Best Psychological Thriller Award, *Suspense Magazine*'s Best Book of 2021 Award, a 2022 Silver Falchion for Best Suspense, and a 2022 Silver Falchion for Best Overall Book of 2021. She grew up in rural western Kentucky and later relocated to Nashville, Tennessee, where she now lives with her husband, daughter, and their two Boston terriers: Cedric and Georgie. Kiersten's work has been translated into multiple languages and readers across the world refer to her as 'The Queen of Twists.' A Netflix addict, Shonda Rhimes superfan, psychology fanatic, and *indoor* enthusiast, Kiersten enjoys rainy days spent with her nose in a book.

Sign up for Kiersten's newsletter here:
kierstenmodglinauthor.com/nlsignup

Sign up for text alerts from Kiersten here:
kierstenmodglinauthor.com/textalerts

kierstenmodglinauthor.com
www.facebook.com/kierstenmodglinauthor
www.facebook.com/groups/kmodsquad
www.twitter.com/kmodglinauthor
www.instagram.com/kierstenmodglinauthor
www.tiktok.com/@kierstenmodglinauthor
www.goodreads.com/kierstenmodglinauthor
www.bookbub.com/authors/kiersten-modglin
www.amazon.com/author/kierstenmodglin

## ALSO BY KIERSTEN MODGLIN

**STANDALONE NOVELS**

Becoming Mrs. Abbott

The List

The Missing Piece

Playing Jenna

The Beginning After

The Better Choice

The Good Neighbors

The Lucky Ones

I Said Yes

The Mother-in-Law

The Dream Job

The Nanny's Secret

The Liar's Wife

My Husband's Secret

The Perfect Getaway

The Roommate

The Missing

Just Married

Our Little Secret

Widow Falls

Missing Daughter

The Reunion

Tell Me the Truth

The Dinner Guests

If You're Reading This...

A Quiet Retreat

**ARRANGEMENT TRILOGY**

The Arrangement (Book 1)

The Amendment (Book 2)

The Atonement (Book 3)

**THE MESSES SERIES**

The Cleaner (The Messes, #1)

The Healer (The Messes, #2)

The Liar (The Messes, #3)

The Prisoner (The Messes, #4)

**NOVELLAS**

The Long Route: A Lover's Landing Novella

The Stranger in the Woods: A Crimson Falls Novella

www.ingramcontent.com/pod-product-compliance
Lightning Source LLC
Chambersburg PA
CBHW030610310726
48979CB00003B/644
* 9 7 8 1 9 5 6 5 3 8 3 3 5 *